ON YOUR OWN

To Greg D'Angelo
With all good wishes
Jonathan Miller

JONATHAN MILLER

This book is a work of fiction. Names, characters, places, and incidents either are products of the author's imagination or are used fictitiously. Any resemblance to actual events or locales or persons, living or dead, is entirely coincidental.

Edited by Joy Tibbs

Cover design by Kevin Brumfield

Cover photo courtesy of the Lexington Herald-Leader

To Jeanne, Suzanne, Rachel and Allison

CONTENTS

ON YOUR OWN

JONATHAN MILLER

Chapter I

Nate watched the college students strolling beneath the tall trees on campus, looking confident and calm. It was late November, so brown leaves dotted the thin layer of frost that covered the grounds. He could see the students' breath, like puffs from a cigarette. The men wore shorts and sweatshirts. The women tied their hair up in ponytails. This was the beginning of everything for them, and they faced it with such indifference.

Nate had neither been confident nor calm at their age. They would go to class and most would work hard, believing that if they made the effort, they would find decent work and be happy. Nate hadn't known what he wanted until he had discovered what he didn't want. Didn't everyone go through that? These students looked like they knew what they wanted, and how to get it.

Nate no longer wanted college or anything it had to offer. He wanted to write, and you don't need school to write. Wendell Berry said to him in a letter, "You need a teacher." So Nate turned to the dead writers. They would be his teachers. But doubt persisted. Was he on the right path?

He wondered how the students could look so confident and calm when he had never been that way. There were some bright-looking students on campus. He could tell by their faces. The sincere faces projected a strong mind. Nate wasn't sure he had a good mind.

The world as he knew it was a sewer. Everything was based on money and he wanted nothing to do with it. There was only one good thing in the world and that was work; and his work was writing. The students, most of them, aspired to work in an office or with a corporation, or to own their own businesses and become wealthy. Nate wanted none of that. The pursuit of wealth did not appeal to him. He wasn't being a snob or a holy man. He liked almost everyone. He would like to work and fight for something, but money wasn't it.

His parents and in-laws and friends – everyone he knew, really – thought his wanting to write was pretty silly. You couldn't make a living at it, they reasoned, and besides, his stories weren't that good. They suggested he write about murder, heroism or villainy, but Nate argued that he wasn't that kind of writer. He had to write what he felt. Nate loved writing so much that their disapproval didn't matter. He loved them even if they didn't respect him.

He wanted to tell the truth: the way life really is. He felt that would be appreciated and valued. His generation might not like that kind of truth-telling, but perhaps the next one and the one that followed would. He didn't care about being abstract or arcane or experimental. Telling the truth would be hard enough.

Life to him was mostly dull. But there were times when he would get nervous, scared, embarrassed or angry, and these emotions would be a jolt. He didn't like them at the time, but when he thought about it later, these were the moments that made life interesting. He would sit down and write what had happened and try to recreate the effect. He could write about actual events or invent ones. Writing was wonderful if he could get the reader to feel the emotion he was describing.

Writing was tough, though. Arranging essential facts to create a real emotion was difficult. Done well, writing was the best business to be in. He couldn't call that kind of writing a business, though, because he didn't think of the financial reward. The only reward was to be accurate; to accurately recreate the good kick he had received from a strong emotion. That was reward enough.

So many of the dead writers were effective in their own way. There wasn't a blueprint to follow. Each cut their own path. That made him want to try his best and attempt to be even better than he was capable of being. Right now, Nate considered himself a good writer. He could be better, but that would come with time. He needed to be alert. He needed to see without judging. He needed to observe and listen. That's all. And read. There was plenty of time to read the greats.

There was one writer he admired the most: Hemingway. His early stories made you feel what life was really like. You could see what the characters saw and feel what they felt. Hemingway captured the rhythm of reality. He made the practice of writing worth living and working and dying for.

No other work could keep Nate's interest the way writing could. It was always a challenge. It also had the best payoff, and the payoff had nothing to do with money. At the end of his life, he would be able to say to himself: "Well, I did what in my heart I loved to do." That was enough.

The college kids would have to find out on their own what was right for them. No one could tell them what was right; they had to find out for themselves. Nate was glad he knew what he wanted. If he asked them now, the college kids would probably say they would like to have an office and make big money and live in the suburbs and have babies. Nate wanted to live in the mountains of Austria or Switzerland. He and his wife could rent a cottage there, and Nate could have his mornings alone to write.

It was always tough getting started. Writing is work, and work is dreaded most of the time. But once he got started he was happy, and when he was done for the day, he would take a walk down the mountain and have a smoke. He would reach a small village and enter a public house, and the bar would be dark and all the furnishings would be made from wood.

The bartender would be old and plump, and he would pour Nate a German wheat beer. Nate would drink it down, and that would help to end the day's work. A farmer would come in and sit next to Nate, and Nate would promise to help him at harvest. Then he would go home and be with his wife and baby for the rest of the afternoon and evening. At night he would think about his writing and wonder whether it was going well. In the early morning he would wake up and think of his writing again. Then he would roll over and hug his wife and kiss her, and tell her how much he loved her and the baby.

He knew as soon as he thought of living that kind of life that it would never happen. It was false. For Nate to write his best stuff, he had to work and live and suffer with other people, and then write about it afterward. Maybe later, when he had enough material, he could work in the mountains. Solitary writing would be the best once he had the material. If he didn't have enough material, he would just be frustrated. Nate could get along anywhere. All he needed to write was paper, some pencils, a pencil sharpener and time. Oh, and an eraser. Yes, always an eraser.

BILLY GOAT'S TAVERN

When Jeremy Burns heard he was going to Chicago, he thought of his grandfather and all the times he had reminisced about what it was like to live there in the old days. He always made the city sound big and tough, and a little intimidating. To a kid it sounded like such a faraway place, like a foreign capital. Burns was sure it was one of the great old cities, where a kid could really learn what was going on in the world.

Burns had never been to a city the size of Chicago. There was so much of the world he wanted to see, but he hadn't seen any of it so far. Most days he stuck to a routine of driving to work and back, passing the same dull houses on the same narrow streets that made up his decaying hometown. Life was slowly and quietly ticking away while, beyond the horizon, a great big world was out there, its inhabitants toasting themselves for the full and exciting lives they were living.

Then one day his wife, Lindy, told him they would be driving the six hours to visit her aunt and uncle who lived in Chicago. He remembered the old black-and-white photographs of Chicago at his grandfather's house. He wondered what the city would look like now and tried to picture himself walking downtown. What a great opportunity it was to actually go somewhere and see something.

They arrived in a neighborhood west of Chicago late on a Friday afternoon. To Burns, the drab houses, the yellow brick apartment building on the corner, and the flat, treeless streets with crisscrossing power lines overhead looked no different from any of the rotten neighborhoods back home. He couldn't even see the Chicago skyline.

Lindy introduced him to her Aunt Annette and Uncle Jack. Aunt Annette asked how long they would be staying and what they would like to do. Burns spoke up. He said that he would very much like to go downtown, to the oldest part of the city. They would be driving back on Sunday, so Saturday would be their only day for sightseeing.

Aunt Annette explained that there was nothing to see downtown; only traffic and crime. She pondered for a moment then smiled at her niece. She spoke of how Lindy had loved the aquarium as a child. Lindy also remembered, and smiled sweetly in response. She agreed that they must see the aquarium while they were there.

"Is it downtown?" Burns asked. Yes, he was assured that it was downtown. *Yes, but is it where all the action is? he wanted to ask.*

The next morning, during the drive downtown, a clear sky revealed the tall, gray, formidable buildings that made up the Chicago skyline. *Wow, look at that*, Burns thought. *The buildings stand shoulder-to-shoulder like a tribute to all human achievement.*

They parked at Soldier Field and headed for the blue water of Lake Michigan. A cool breeze blew off the lake, making him forget how hot the sun felt. Burns spotted a sailboat far out on the glittering lake. He took one last look at the sparkling water and the tall buildings on the south side before entering the aquarium.

Once inside, they were forced to stop behind a long line of parents and children. A mother held and patted her screaming baby while her older children broke away to see what was holding up the line. They were waiting for the first dark hallway to clear. People crammed in close to one another in the hall, staring at the lighted tanks along the wall.

When they finally entered the hall, Burns stood on tiptoes to peer over the many heads to see the tanks. Small fish darted swiftly and smoothly, then stopped at one end to run their noses along the glass. *Look, they want out*, he thought.

He and the other family members followed the crowd from tank to tank. Burns fell behind before excusing himself back out of the hall and into an open area in the middle of the building. He checked his watch. *This is our only day of sightseeing, too*, he thought.

This wasn't the Chicago he had heard about. That big, bustling city was right outside. He thought of his grandfather. He remembered him saying that he had been living in Louisville when his cousin had invited him up to Chicago to watch a ballgame at Wrigley Field. His cousin said they would have the day to themselves, and could stay out all night and just have a grand time in the city.

His grandfather went to work the next day and told his boss he would not be in the following Monday. The boss told him if he didn't show up for work on Monday he would be fired. The next Monday his grandfather took a train to Chicago anyway. He and his cousin watched the Cubs play at Wrigley Field, then headed into the city for drinks. And this was during Prohibition. He moved in with his cousin and they lived together for two years. That's how long it took him to get homesick for Louisville.

When he returned to his hometown he was out of work, so he went to his old workplace and peeked in at the boss' window. The boss yelled, "Lester! Is that you? Where the hell have you been?"

His grandfather told him he had been in Chicago, working at a canning factory. The boss asked him to sit down and tell him all he had seen and done. After a while, the boss asked if he needed a job. Burns' grandfather had said that he did, and he was hired back a week later.

Burns could hear his grandfather's voice: "Well, it wasn't too smart to up and leave your job like that. But I was just a kid and we had more good times in Chicago. It was some town."

One time his grandfather had been in his cousin's apartment when he heard two men shouting in the alley. He stuck his head out the window and saw one of the men pull out a gun and point it at the other.

The man being held up smarted off: "Put that thing away. That ain't nothing but a cap gun."

"Don't bet on it," the man with the gun said.

The man being held up reached for the gun, when it went off with a "Pow!" He checked himself for holes, then grabbed the gun away and began beating the other man over the head with it.

"What's the matter with you?!" he shouted, still beating him.

Burns was willing to bet his grandfather never wasted time at an aquarium. He checked his watch again. All the excitement about being in Chicago was gone. The trip had gone to hell. *What have you ever seen or done in your life?* he asked himself. He drew a blank. *Congratulations; you're one dull SOB. You don't mean to be, it's just turned out that way.*

He looked back toward the dark hall, and when his eyes adjusted to the darkness he could see Lindy and her aunt standing together, her aunt pointing at something in the tank. *How do you expect to see anything tagging along with those birds?* he thought.

Standing guard behind the women was Uncle Jack, who looked like an old bone. His arms were crossed over his big gut and he stood there looking big and immovable. Burns bet the old man knew plenty about the city. He had lived here all his life. He bet Uncle Jack could show him around. The old man turned and spotted Burns standing outside the hall and started toward him. He was red-faced, wore thick, black-framed glasses, had a full head of white hair and breathed hard just from walking.

He came up to Burns: "Are you lost?"

Burns hesitated and considered it a deeper question than was probably intended. "Yes, I suppose I am."

"Having a good time?"

"Sure."

"The girls seem to be having a good time," the old man said, looking back at them in the hall.

"It was their idea," Burns said.

The old man looked at him. "Do you want to get out of here?"

"No, it's fine."

"Is there something else you'd like to do?"

"I was hoping we could go downtown."

"Where the hell do you think we are?"

"I meant I thought we would see downtown."

"We're getting to it. Don't you worry. Would you rather we left now?"

"Just you and me?"

"Yeah," the old man said. "Come on. I know where we can get a drink. Wait. Let me go tell the girls."

Burns waited by the steps that went down to the front of the building. When the old man came back, Burns asked if they had put up a fight.

"Lindy didn't look too happy. I knew not to look at Annie."

"I'm dead."

"Oh, come on," the old man said dismissively, waving at him to follow. "I told them we'd have one drink."

The old man jostled through the crowd at the front of the aquarium with Burns in his wake. To reach the car they had to walk under the street through a tunnel. The last two steps that led into the tunnel were shaded and the smell of something rotten drifted out. Burns took a deep breath and then held it.

"What's that smell?" Burns' voice was strained.

"What smell?" the old man asked.

Burns blew out his breath and took a whiff. The foul odor was still there and growing thicker, like a mix of skunk and old urine. He shut down his nose and breathed through his mouth.

There was a constant roar of cars passing overhead. They came upon a man with a scraggly beard, wearing a long overcoat and dark glasses, and playing a violin. He worked the bow slowly over the strings. It was a sad song. On the ground beside him lay an open violin case with bills folded over and coins scattered inside. Burns stopped and reached into his pocket. The old man slapped his leg and grunted.

Once they were out of the tunnel, the old man said: "You don't want to do that. He's one of the richest men in the city. It's a scam."

"How do you know he's rich?"

"Hell, he has a mansion in Wisconsin and a big cabin in Minnesota. Everyone around here knows that."

"Is he really blind?"

"Nope."

Burns wondered if the man really made that kind of money. *Boy, that'd be something if you could get rich that way.*

When they reached the parking lot, Burns couldn't stop staring at the immense stone structure of Soldier Field looming over them. It looked like the oldest, most important football stadium of all time.

"You don't want to be around here on the day of a game," the old man said. "It's a madhouse."

"I'd love to go to a Bears game. I like being out in the crowd."

"Ha! You don't know what a crowd is. I'll show you a crowd. Get in."

Traffic was heavy around the stadium. The old man whipped the car back and forth, in and out of lanes, narrowly missing bumpers. Cars were making their own lanes. He screamed at locals, out-of-towners, cabbies and pedestrians. When he stuck his head out the window to yell, the wind whipped his feathery hair out of place. His left arm stayed outside the window; he used it to wave people to move on, stop, hurry up, or slow down.

The old man backhanded him in the chest. "People here drive with their heads up their asses. They think only of themselves. They have no concern for other cars on the road. When you drive you should be conscious of everyone around you. The road wasn't built especially for you. Understand?"

The traffic was particularly heavy due to a parade that was going on in one section. The city was saluting the Irish potato farmers who had migrated from New York at the turn of the twentieth century.

"If you work hard and try to raise a family and keep your trap shut, Chicago will throw you a parade," the old man said. "Everyone should shoot for a parade. We should go see it. You want to see the parade?"

"Sure."

The old man tapped the brake and peered down a narrow street, where cars were parked on both sides.

"Dammit! Should have turned there. Oh well, we're going to Billy Goat's. That's where we were headed."

Burns could hear trumpets and drums, and a crowd cheering and whistling. He craned his neck, hoping to catch a glimpse of the marchers, but all he saw at the end of a long side street was a portion of the crowd standing between two buildings. As they drove on, the parade sounded farther and farther away. Burns felt his heart leap. This was the Chicago he wanted to see. *Now this is exciting*, he thought.

The old man pulled into a parking garage across the street from the IBM building. He nodded at the tall, black glass building without looking at it. He mentioned that he once had an office on the thirty-eighth floor. Burns counted up thirty-eight windows. "I see your floor."

They cut around the corner of another building and came up alongside the Chicago River. Walking along the river, they had a good view of the many buildings and the various architectural styles. Burns liked the oldest buildings best. He looked over his shoulder to catch the movement of the river. The green water surged and dipped and rocked quietly toward

a bridge. The waves never toppled over like ocean surf. The old man said
gangsters had used the river all the time in the old days.

"To take a leak?" Burns asked.

"No. They dumped double-crossers in there."

Burns wondered why anyone would risk double-crossing a gangster.
He wished they would pass a few gangsters on the sidewalk. He wondered
what they looked like.

They reached a flight of stairs that led below street level. A whole new
world was alive beneath the street. It was like a cave: dark and open and
echoey. There were still traffic lights and side streets, but there was a lot
less commotion. Burns followed the old man down a pitch-black side lane.
They walked deeper and deeper until there was no longer any light, either
before them or behind. If it hadn't been for the sound of the old man's
shoes scratching and scraping the pavement, Burns would have felt lost.
Then, up ahead, a bright red-and-white sign appeared.

"There's Billy Goat's!" the old man's voice echoed.

"Wow," Burns said. "Billy Goat's."

The old man opened the door to the tavern. Inside was a sunken room
with a U-shaped counter in the center. Behind the counter, young men
in black T-shirts wrapped sandwiches and stuffed them into white sacks.
Smoke rose from the grill behind them. The place smelled of grilled ham-
burgers and onions. They stepped down and turned right, heading for
the long bar that took up the front right side. One bartender wore a gray
T-shirt, his arms covered with curly black hair. The other bartender was
short and bald, with deep creases in his face.

The old man sat down on a stool at the bar and shouted much louder
than he needed to. "Have a seat, Burns! What'll you have?!"

"Whatever's on tap."

"That'll be Schlitz, then. Two Schlitz drafts," the old man hollered,
slapping the bar. The bartender with the hairy arms nodded seriously.

The old man waited for the bartender to turn around, then said to
Burns: "This is the only place in the world, I believe, that has Schlitz on
tap. Long ago, Schlitz and Budweiser used to slug it out for most beer sales.
Now Schlitz isn't even in the running. But Billy Goat's won't change. They
keep it the same as it was in the forties."

Burns had always heard Schlitz was skunk beer, but he didn't say anything. *I'll drink it and decide for myself,* he thought. He watched the bartender slide open the cooler door behind the bar and take out two icy mugs. He put the mugs under the Schlitz tap and drew the beer.

The old man smiled reminiscently. "I used to come down here every night after work," he said. "That was when this place was a good little joint. You could come in here and have a drink with the Bears coaches or whatever bigwig was in town. You won't see anyone here now except tourists.

"We had some good times here, though. After the kids were born, I had to cut it all out. The old lady didn't like me stopping here after work. Said she needed help with the kids and all. I fought her off as long as I could. Then one day she said I had to make a decision. It wasn't much of a decision. I knew what I had to do. Hell, I almost cut out drinking altogether. I don't drink like I used to. If I never have another, I've had more than my share."

Burns swung around to look at the place. Beyond the hamburger counter at the other side of the room were photographs and portraits of men all along the wall, along with framed clippings of newspaper articles.

"Who are those pictures of over there?" Burns pointed to the far wall.

The old man mentioned the name Royko and various other newspapermen. He pointed to a picture of the tavern's dead owner with his trademark goatee. Then he explained the picture of the owner standing with a goat and surrounded by police in front of Wrigley Field.

The owner had wanted to walk the goat onto the field for good luck when the Cubs played the Tigers in the 1945 World Series. A newspaper article quoted the owner saying, "We've got Detroit's goat."

But the Cubs wouldn't allow him or the goat onto the field, and when he protested, he was arrested. The owner put a hex on the Cubs for treating him so shabbily. The Cubs lost the Series and have not made it back to the World Series since.

"So that's why they're so bad," Burns said, swinging back around to face the bar. Sitting a few seats down from them were several older, stubble-faced, badly dressed men watching the Notre Dame-Northwestern football game on a television above the bar. Nobody in the room looked like a bigwig. Burns wished someone important would come in.

The bartender set two large, icy mugs of beer on the bar in front of them. Burns grabbed the mug, brought it quickly to his lips and turned it up. He tried to down the beer, but it was too cold. The beer froze his teeth and his eyes began to water. Schlitz tasted fine to Burns.

He nudged the old man in the arm. "I want to thank you for bringing me here. This is great. I mean *really* great."

The old man lifted his mug towards him, winked and took a drink.

"I wish we didn't have to leave," Burns said. "You know, you remind me a little of my grandfather. You've both had some good times here in Chicago. I haven't done anything." He turned around in his seat to admire the pictures on the wall and the bustle in the bar.

The old man took another drink.

Burns elbowed him again in the arm. "Say! What if we hang out here the rest of the day?"

The old man didn't respond. He was letting Burns carry the conversation while he drank.

Burns elbowed him again. "We'll tell Lindy and Annette we've decided to stay here. We'll let them have the car. That way they can go wherever they want."

All right, the old man thought, *he's getting a little carried away. Poor kid must never get out.*

"You know it?" Burns elbowed him again for a response. "Let's hang out here all night. The women can take the car."

The old man was hoping the kid would run out of gas.

"What do you say?" Burns moved his head in closer to gauge the old man's reaction. "Huh?"

The old man made a strange face.

"What?" Burns said.

"Don't be silly."

"Why not?"

The old man finally looked at Burns. His sour expression was not encouraging. "Oh, don't be a weenie. You're asking for trouble. I told the girls we'd have one drink and that's what we're doing. Now finish that up," he pointed at Burns' beer. "If Lindy wants to come back here, fine." He tapped his fingernail on the bar for emphasis.

Burns was stunned. He thought he had found a companion. He responded sadly. "She won't. She hates beer and she hates bars and it bothers her that I like both."

"Well, then, we'll get into something else."

"No, we won't."

The old man watched Burns' jawbone twitch from grinding his teeth. *Look at him*, he thought. He didn't like the young man's silly suffering. He finished his beer and scooted the mug forward.

"Well, this was nice. Haven't been in here for a long time. Come on," the old man stood up and patted Burns on the shoulder. "Let's go get the girls and see what they want to do."

Burns remained seated.

The old man walked over to the steps. He was about to start up them when he looked back and saw that Burns hadn't budged. *I wonder what's going on in that silly head of his*, he thought.

Burns finished off his beer, set his mug forward and stood up. *I guess I can decide for myself when it's time to leave. He's not going to tell me. I could hang out here all night. How's he going to stop it? If I wanted to sit here for the next couple of years, how's anyone going to stop it?*

Chapter II

"Oh, no!" Mother said from the kitchen.

"What?" Father asked from his chair in the living room. I was sitting across from him on the couch watching baseball on TV. Rosemary, my mother's sister – an old Southern lady – was on the floor playing with my one-year-old, Katy.

"You're going to kill me," Mother said.

"What did you do?" Father asked, sounding irritated.

"You're going to kill me."

"Did you burn the liver?"

"No."

"We're going to kill you if you don't tell us," I said jokingly, trying to tamp down the rising tension.

"I'm dead," she said sadly.

"Did you burn the beans again?" Father jumped up and rushed into the kitchen. I heard him lift the pot lid.

"Damn you!" he shouted, throwing the lid onto the stove. It bounced off and fell to the floor.

"Watch it, watch it," Mother said. "That almost hit Marie."

My oldest daughter, Marie, aged three, was standing in the middle of the kitchen floor, watching.

"I don't believe you!"

"I know, I know. I'm sorry."

"You're sorry, all right."

Rosemary shook her head and said my father's name in a voice that was louder than a whisper: "Ben Owen."

"What's the matter with you?" he continued. "The beans again. You do this all the time. Damn you!"

I could picture Marie looking up at her grandpa as he yelled and scolded her grandma, whom she loved with all her heart.

Rosemary looked at me: "Why don't you tell him to shut up?"

I didn't answer. I was watching the Reds bat with runners on first and third. I hoped my father would end the tirade on his own and soon.

"You can't do nothing right," he said.

Now that was a lie, I thought. Mother was a very good cook. She might be overworked, which caused some mistakes, but she could not be accused of doing nothing right. But if my father wants to yell at my mother, it's his call. I'm not interfering in their marriage.

"I'm sorry. Everything you say is right," Mother said pitifully.

"I know you're sorry. Very sorry."

Rosemary spoke up this time. "Katy, close your ears."

There was a pause in the house. Everyone listened for my father's reaction in the kitchen. He took a step that made the floor groan.

Rosemary said it again. "Katy, close your ears."

I could feel my father's anger rising as he heard this second volley.

"And you can shut your mouth in there," he yelled at Rosemary.

"What?" Mother said. "She was talking to Katy."

"I know what she's doing. I don't need her two cents' worth."

Rosemary puffed up her cheeks and stared out the window. She was probably deciding what weapon to use.

The kitchen door opened from the driveway, and in came my wife, Beth, who was just returning from work. The house fell silent. Father was done.

My wife looked at me, aware of the strange silence. "What? What happened?"

"Nothing," I lied.

After the storm, my father settled into his chair in front of the TV. Beth and I were in the kitchen, fixing a plate for Marie, when we saw her walk into the living room.

We heard her say to her grandpa, "Are you going to apologize to Namaw?"

"Me?" Father said.

"You have to apologize."

"Leave it alone," he said.
"But …"
"Leave it alone."
"Marie, come in here," I said.
I thought, Damn, Marie has a lot more guts than I do.

THE PREACHER'S SON

The best part of the day for Steve Burdon was late afternoon, when he got out of his last class. He would cut across the heart of campus – each step taking him farther and farther away from his classmates gathering at the student center – to reach the sidewalk that led to Main Street. There he would pass his father's church and continue three more blocks to reach the outskirts of town to his apartment. School and town were left behind.

On a late afternoon in early fall, Steve lay on the couch in the living room and looked out through the glass patio door at the tall grass blowing in the field. After a few blinks the field became an open sea. There was an empty raft floating on the sea, so he put himself on it. He closed his eyes and felt the waves rising and falling.

There was no shoreline in sight; only flat sea and blue sky wherever he looked. He leaned over the side and looked into the green water. Maybe when he awoke, he would be somewhere he had never been before. He would like that.

A ringing noise, like the jangling of small bells, made him sit up on the raft. Was someone sounding an alert on the sea? The ring came again, louder this time. He was no longer on the raft. He was back on the couch in his apartment. The ringing continued, blaring out in measured intervals.

I know what that is, he thought. *That's the damn phone.* He instinctively rolled off the couch. It sounded urgent and serious in his newly awakened state. He gripped the phone severely.

"Hello!"

"Steve? Oh, Steve, I'm glad I caught you." It was his girlfriend, Regina.

"What do you want?"

"What do I want? I don't want anything."

"I'm sorry, sweetheart. I didn't mean it that way."

"Am I bothering you?"

"Of course not."

"Well, you'd be nice to me if you knew how upset I was. I just got off the phone with my sister. We were talking, and she mentioned your dad."

She paused.

"What about him?"

"She just told me something."

"What?"

"Oh, Steve. I can't say it."

"Just say it. What is it?"

"Please don't make me say it."

"What's it about, then?"

"Do you know a woman at your church named Leatha?"

The air went out of him. Hearing that name was always a kick in the stomach. Regina saying it was worse.

"Yes, I know her."

"Please tell me it's not true."

"What are you talking about?"

"So it's not true?"

"I don't even know what you're saying."

"Well, that makes me feel better."

"Well, I'm happy for you."

"Please don't be that way. I'm sorry I brought it up."

"No, it's fine. Call any time."

"Please don't be cruel."

"I'm hanging up now."

"Why are you doing this?"

Click. He hung up the phone and unplugged the cord from the jack. He went back to the couch and lay down again. He was wide awake now, and a little in shock. *If Regina's sister has heard, someone in the congregation must know. And if someone in the congregation knows, at least half the congregation knows. Jeez.*

He shook his head. *And you. What have you done? You haven't done a damn thing. Why? Why haven't you tried to talk to him? Because it's a hell of a thing to bring up to your father, that's why. How the hell do you discuss that? Why don't you ask God for help? God will give you strength. He would want you to at least make the effort.*

He sat up and put his head in his hands, trying to think of a way to approach his father. An idea struck. *I got it. How about this? You don't accuse him of anything. You're just a messenger. You say, "Here's what the talk is ... I thought you'd want to know what the church is saying." Yeah. That's it.*

He closed his eyes, hoping for a sleepy feeling. *But why hasn't someone else confronted him? Why do I have to do it? How the hell am I going to say that to him? I'll chicken out.*

He tried to put it out of his mind, but it wouldn't go away. His father's world was about to blow up. And he, his only son, was standing in the crowd, watching the fuse burn. He hadn't done anything to help him. He was just a spectator. He could potentially end this thing now if he could tell him how much pain he's causing. *Just try, dammit! Talk to him. Just talk to him!*

He sat up and reached for his watch on the coffee table. It read six thirty-five. *If I leave now I could reach Leatha's house while Dad is still there. Make it brief and then get the hell out. I can't let this fester any longer. Hyenas are starting to gather outside the parsonage.*

Outside, the weather had turned cold; much too cold for his shorts and T-shirt. Taking the walkway behind the apartment complex, he passed the swimming pool, which had been drained and covered. A padlock hung from the gate.

Daylight had failed to the point that he could see only the outline of trees and the buildings on Main Street. The patch of sky above him looked like cigarette smoke. Walking under buzzing streetlights, he passed a market, a liquor store and a topless joint. The red sign with the three Xs flickered on. The red light cast a seductive glow at night.

He had to cross busy Main Street to reach the new subdivision where Leatha lived. Cars waiting at the light seemed to know what he was up to. He kept his head down and tried to concentrate on a plan. He could picture himself stepping into the front room, saying, 'The reason I'm here is …' But that would be as far as he could get. There was nothing more he could think of to say.

He walked alongside a fence bordering an empty field that was waiting to be developed. A mouse on the sidewalk scampered for the fence, dipped under it and disappeared into the field. At the end of the field was the entrance to Leatha's subdivision. It was six blocks of three-bedroom ranch houses on small lots. On reaching the entrance, he continued as if he were really going to go through with it.

A cold wind raised goosebumps on his arms. He started up a steep hill that had an even sharper climb at the top. Halfway up he felt the heaviness of his weight. Sweat beaded on his forehead. He was freezing and sweating at the same time. It angered him.

You buck-toothed, scrawny, veiny, thick-glasses-wearing, saggy, small-breasted, floppy-footed, prematurely-gray-hair-cut-short-like-a-lesbian witch. Would it be OK if she were beautiful? he asked himself. *At least you could understand it. You would say he was weak and undisciplined. What do you say now? Pathetic?*

He reached the top of the hill. Leatha's house was on the second street on the left; the second house on the right. The sky was almost completely dark now. Not one porch light was on in the neighborhood. It was shut up for the night. The streetlights lit the way.

He felt himself getting nervous. *God, what am I doing here? I can't go through with this. Oh, shut up. You've come this far. Remember, you don't have to accuse anyone of anything. Just say what the talk is. That a rumor is going around and it may have reached the congregation. It's only a matter of time before the rumor reaches Mom.* He thought about his mother. His poor, pitiful mother.

He had never had a conversation with her about it. Once, when he had asked her what she thought of Leatha, she had looked shocked that her name would be mentioned in the house. She had turned around to face the sink, even though there were no dirty dishes in it. She had run the water anyway and then turned the faucet off. She had tried to change the subject by asking if he had brought his dirty clothes home to be washed.

When he had mentioned Leatha again, she had played dumb, as if she refused to comprehend the implication. She acted the same way he had acted when Regina called. As they stood there, neither one offering to pursue the matter any further, Steve thought he saw the hurt setting in. She seemed to be struggling internally. Seeing her hurting so made him angry. After that, he had never had the will to press her about it again.

He always wondered if she had found out or if she just suspected. The women in the church who came to the house regularly would probably never confront her about the matter. They would talk among themselves, no doubt. Mom had every right to grab Dad by the throat and shake some sense into him, but she was too weak and intimidated by him. He knew his mother would never do that. He felt vaguely sympathetic.

After seeing her reaction, he wanted to rush to his father and curse him to his face. He had gone to his dad's office the next day, something he never, ever did. It was awkward sitting on the other side of the desk from him in the middle of the day, as though he were conducting church business. He couldn't summon the outrage from the day before. He groped around for an excuse for dropping by, then, once outside, he scolded himself for his miserable performance. He decided then that he could never look his father in the eye and ask about Leatha.

Yet here he was, within shouting distance of her house, shivering from the cold and trying to force himself to confront them. *You have to try something or everything will go to hell. Wouldn't God be disappointed if you didn't help your own family?*

A junky, muffler-less pickup truck rumbled into the subdivision. Steve turned around and saw the truck's headlights coming toward him, so he ran over to hide in the shadow between two houses. He watched the truck turn left onto Leatha's street, barking the tires in the turn. He could see the whole of Leatha's house: the one little tree in the front yard and her red two-door compact car parked at the bottom of the driveway. There was another car in front of hers, parked as far up as it could go. Most of the car was hidden, but the back end looked a lot like his dad's sedan.

Steve stepped out from the houses and squatted behind one of the trees between the sidewalk and the street. *Well, shit. Am I going over there or not?* He watched Leatha's house, hoping to see some activity. All the windows were dark, like all the other houses. *Damn, does everyone just sit in the dark in this neighborhood?*

The rough-sounding truck was already a block away. He could hear each turn it made and watched as it came back to Leatha's street. This time the truck slowed as it passed her house, then sped on. The truck circled four times by Steve's count, slowing each time at Leatha's house.

I know that truck. That's Duane's truck. What's he doing going round and round his mother's house? I thought he was at school in Florida.

He remembered reading in the church bulletin about a year ago that Duane was leaving to go live with his father in Florida and would be attending college there. But it was the middle of the school semester, and he was back home circling his mother's house.

Duane's truck squealed to a stop at the end of Leatha's driveway, the motor left idling. Duane jumped down and ran around to the back of the house. Steve heard the back door open and close. *Oh, no. Oh, no.*

Watching the house very carefully, Steve's eyes darted from the front door to the large front window and the curtain, which was drawn all the way across. There were no lights turned on inside that he could tell, and there was no evidence that Duane's entrance had made an impact. The house remained quiet. Then came a *boom-boom-boom* from what sounded like a cannon. There was no mistaking the sound of gunfire. The report was heavy and swift.

Steve looked around the neighborhood to see what the reaction would be to that God-awful sound. A dog started barking, then another and another. But nothing stirred from inside the houses. When he looked back at Leatha's, he saw Duane running down the driveway, carrying something in his hand. He opened the truck door with one hand and flipped what was in his other hand into the passenger's seat. He turned the truck around in the street, then gunned the engine. It rattled so loudly Steve thought it was about to fall out. Dogs were barking like mad now.

Steve jumped up like a spring and took off running toward Leatha's house. He couldn't feel his legs or the pavement. He was there in an instant and leaped onto the front porch. He reached for the door handle, then decided that was a bad idea. He leaned into the railing to peep into the corner of the window where the curtain didn't quite reach. All he could see was the leg of a chair and the carpet beneath. It was too dark in the house. He listened for any noise, but there was none. Not even the chatter of a TV.

He jumped down and ran around to the driveway. The car parked in front was indeed his dad's. He knelt down and leaned his back against his dad's car. *What if they're still alive? What if they need help?* He dropped his head into his hands. *Oh, you can't go in there. There's no telling what you'll see. There's no way.* He didn't want to move, but he knew he must get out of there.

Steve shot straight down the driveway, crossed the street and cut through a neighbor's yard so he wouldn't be seen running under the street-lights. It seemed as though every dog in the neighborhood was barking. The wailing sirens of an ambulance and a police car could be heard on Main Street, getting closer all the time.

He cut through the backyards, finding enough fenceless properties to beat it out of the subdivision. He was running so fast that it was impossible to avoid the tree limbs that slapped his face and arms. *If he could just reach his apartment, he could think things through. If he could just reach his apartment.*

He ran through the open field, then stayed at the back of the businesses that were on the same street as his apartment. He made it into his place, choking, stomach-cramping and unable to catch his breath. His face was flushed, and flecked with blood and sweat. He was suddenly burning up and sweat poured down his face. He went into the bathroom, took off his clothes and showered. The many cuts from the tree limbs stung on contact with the hot water.

He wrapped a towel around his waist, went into the living room and sat down on the couch. He tried to cry but nothing came out. He couldn't feel anything. That would have to come later. He saw the phone on the kitchen table and the cord, which was still unplugged from the jack, lying on the floor. He decided that a couple more minutes unplugged would be nice.

Chapter III

All the parents came forward and picked up their children, hurrying them out so the next Christmas program could begin. We got our daughter, Eve, in the car and started for home. I couldn't leave the crummy church fast enough.

Eve was developmentally delayed, at least a year behind her peers. Did we have to stick her in a Christmas program and expose her shortcomings to the world? My wife argued that Eve wanted to perform for her parents like all the other kids.

The night had been a miserable failure, and I could think of nothing else. It had started with Eve crying after her hat with the reindeer antlers fell off her head onto the stage. The other kids just looked at her and continued singing.

Later on she had broken line when she spotted her mother and, while stepping forward to reach for her, had fallen off the stage. But the music director had given her a chance to save face by waiting for her to recover. Once Eve had composed herself, she was walked back onto the stage with the others – to a rousing ovation.

But she had held out her arms for her mother and started to cry again, unable to finish the program without her mother by her side.

"No other kid needed their mother," I said to my wife.

"That's OK," she said.

"But she's a year older than them."

"No she's not. That was the two-year-olds."

"I thought she would be singing with her class."

"No. There's no program for ones. The music director thought Eve was good enough to sing with the twos."

"Are you serious?"

"Yes."

"I didn't know that. Well, that changes everything."

I turned this latest development over and over in my head. She had achieved something that had previously been unattainable. Just five months earlier, she wasn't ready to be in class with kids her age, so they had moved her back to the ones. She couldn't even walk to the lunchroom on her own. A kid much younger than her had held her hand and led her everywhere the class went. But in music, they thought she had caught up.

"It's like being called up to the big leagues," I said. "Granted, she dropped her helmet, struck out and was hit by a pitch. But hey ..."

"Would you stop with the sports analogy?" my wife laughed.

"They thought enough of her to promote her to the bigs." I turned around and tapped her on the knee. "Way to go, kid."

"Guk," said Eve.

That's her word for milk.

"OK, when we get home."

She was trying. She was achieving. She was doing the best she could. That's all we can ask of her. Or of anyone, really.

FIRST DAY OF SCHOOL

The night before the first day of school, Fitz told Nate how much fun first grade was going to be. He would have his own desk and his own pencils, crayons, paper and glue. The work wouldn't be very hard. He would memorize and write the alphabet, capital letters and small letters. "That's about it," Fitz said. "And learn to read. The best part is recess. There'll be kickball, or you could swing or climb on the monkey bars."

As he listened to Fitz, Nate jumped up and down on his knees on the bed and pretended to pant like a dog. He couldn't wait to go to school.

In the morning, the boys' mother came into the room and awoke them by singing "School Days." It was just like a church morning, when Nate's sleep was interrupted for Sunday school.

He hated waking up for Sunday school, and now he didn't want to get up for first grade. Everything Fitz had said the night before was forgotten. Nate thought of the enormous five-story school building, which looked like a penitentiary, and of all the grown-ups and children that would be there. He wanted to sleep in. He wanted to have breakfast later on with his mom. He wanted to play with Fitz's army men. He would set up battles in every room in the house when Fitz was at school. He wanted to swing on his swing set in the backyard in the afternoon and chase the robins that landed in the yard. School could never be better than all that.

"Wake up, angel," his mother said sweetly. "You've got great things to do today."

"I'll be down in a minute," he replied.

After his mother headed downstairs, Nate went back to sleep. He awoke to the sound of voices coming from the backyard. He got up, walked over to the window and opened it. Fog had settled in; it was almost touching the grass. Fitz and someone else were up close to the house, out of sight.

"Can you believe they put us in homeroom together again?" It was the voice of Fitz's friend Jason. He lived two streets over.

"Yeah, I can't believe it."

"I bet Mrs. Bowman can't paddle a bit. She's so old. Mr. Hall can paddle, though," Jason said.

"Yeah," Fitz said. "Well, I gotta go back inside. I'll see you at school."

"Don't you want to walk together?"

"I have to walk Nate to first grade."

"Oh, why can't your mom do it?"

"She asked me to. She said it might go better if I take him."

"Oh, that stinks."

"Want to walk with us?"

"No. I ain't walking to school with no first-grader."

"Well, I'll see you at homeroom then."

"All right."

Nate heard Fitz walking up the steps at the back of the house. He dressed and went downstairs, where his mother was fixing him a bowl of cereal. She put it down on the kitchen table.

"You'll have to hurry with your cereal, honey, Fitz is waiting," his mother said. "I let you sleep later than I should have. Tomorrow if you get up early, I'll fix you a big breakfast."

"Mom," Nate said, feeling an ache in his throat, "I don't want to go to school."

"Oh, honey, it'll be fine. You'll meet lots of kids your age and make new friends."

"I don't want to meet any kids."

"Oh, sweetie, you have to go to school. We want you to learn. And you'll have so much fun if you just give it a chance."

Fitz walked into the kitchen. "Ready to go, Nate?" he asked.

Nate felt like he was going to cry. He didn't want Fitz to see it, so he held it off.

"We've got to go, Mom," Fitz said.

"All right, honey," she said, moving towards Nate. "Hop down now. You just stay with Fitz, OK? He'll show you to your classroom."

"OK."

"I want you to be strong today. If you get sad or upset or if you miss home, remember you're only there for a little while. You'll be back home before you know it."

"OK."

She handed Nate his lunchbox and walked out with them as far as the sidewalk.

"Good luck, boys," she said, watching as they crossed the street. They cut between two houses, taking the worn path beside a tall hedgerow. Her eyes filled up and a single drop spilled over and ran down the side of her nose. She raised a hand to cover her mouth.

Nate liked walking with Fitz. For the first time ever, he felt that he and his brother were pals. They cut through their neighbor's yard and came out onto a wide driveway that separated two houses. At the house on the right, they saw a man sitting on the porch tying his shoes. The man jumped off the porch and headed for his car on the street. He was wearing a suit, as though he were going to church.

"Say, boys, you're lucky you get to go to school," the man said. "I have to go to work."

Fitz laughed.

Nate heard the metallic clunk of a garbage truck at the bottom of Brown Street. A skinny fellow was hanging off the back of the truck. As it came to a stop he jumped down, ran to the curb and picked up a garbage can. He flung the lid into the yard and then tossed the can carelessly into the back of the truck. After shaking the can vigorously a couple times, he slung it back into the yard. Then he pulled a lever to crush the trash and jumped on the back of the truck, reaching for the handrail at the same time. The truck continued down the street.

That looks like fun, Nate thought.

Fourth Street led to the back of the school. Nate knew this, but he was trying to put it out of his mind. He and Fitz jumped into a grassy ditch next to the road. On the right was an empty yard that Nate decided would be perfect for football and Wiffle ball and kickball.

At the bottom of Fourth Street, they passed Flynn Lane. Nate looked up the steep, narrow, treacherous street with its rickety porches and small houses, which leaned to one side. Towels, rags and sheets hung from a clothesline in a side yard. A bare-chested man with a pot belly stood on one of the porches smoking the stub of a cigar. He leaned over the rail and spat a big glob into the street.

Nate turned away, afraid that the man was about to shout at him.

Straight ahead was a small climb to a stop sign and beyond the stop sign was the back of the school. A policeman stood in the intersection, waving kids across the street. Nate felt a sick emptiness in his stomach. They were almost there.

Then came a *bam!* Nate's lunchbox rattled in his hand. The lid opened and its contents spilled out onto the road. The sandwich fell flat, the apple and Thermos rolling until they stopped at the curb. Fitz saw a big rock spin and stop in the middle of the street. He looked all around him before spotting Jason up ahead. Jason ran out from behind a pine tree, laughing.

"Jason!" Fitz shouted and started after him.

"Fitz, don't go!" Nate said, squatting down to gather his things.

Fitz hurried over to Nate and knelt down next to him. He could see that his brother was trying not to cry.

"The bread has rocks in it," Nate said, brushing them off.

"That's OK," Fitz said. "Jason was trying to hit me with that rock."

"I'll hit *him* with a rock."

"No, I'll get him."

One side of the lunchbox had a big, dented crease that was so severe it wouldn't close, so Nate had to carry it with both hands. Fitz put an arm around Nate and told him Mom and Dad would get him another lunchbox.

When they arrived at the school, Fitz and Nate walked down a crowded hallway. Fitz read the names of the teachers outside each classroom. There were so many kids running about. Nate couldn't believe there were that many kids his age running around in the world.

Fitz found Mrs. Jones' room and told Nate she was his homeroom teacher.

"What do I do?" Nate asked.

"Just go in and sit down at one of the desks," Fitz replied. "She'll probably seat everyone in alphabetical order later on."

"Will you go in with me?"

"I can't. I have to go to my class."

"Where is it?"

"Upstairs. I've got to go now. Listen, if you miss home or anything, just remember that at three o'clock I'll meet you here. So if things are going bad, just remember three o'clock. It's not that far off. We'll go home and play. OK?"

"OK," Nate said. He watched Fitz run down the hall and disappear around a corner.

Nate stood in the embrasure of the doorway. He saw Mrs. Jones sitting behind a desk, reading. She was wearing glasses with a chain attached to them. She was old and had a large nest of black and gray hair. There was a red pen tucked behind her ear. Her face was stern. Not mean, but not pleasant either.

Nate peeked into the room to see what the rest of the class looked like. Just about every desk was filled with odd-looking girls and boys. Mrs. Jones twisted her head toward Nate. Her lips moved, but there was so much noise out in the hallway he couldn't hear what she was saying. She beckoned him over.

He shook his head and ran off down the hallway toward the exit. When he reached the double doors he pressed his back into the left-hand door and found himself outside.

Nate spotted the policeman standing on the corner and walked up to him.

"The school's that way, little man," the policeman said. He was fat and black and had the sweetest, kindest smile Nate had ever seen.

"I know. I forgot something at home. I just live down the street."

"OK, but hurry up. You don't want to be late on your first day."

Nate crossed the street and then took off running, holding onto his broken lunchbox with both hands. Nate thought the policeman was watching him, so he ran down Fourth Street until he was out of sight.

At Brown Street he spotted a robin standing in the road. It looked at Nate and cocked its head to one side, as if to say, "Why aren't you at home, chasing me in the backyard?"

"I'm going there now," Nate answered. "Come on, follow me."

Nate emerged from the tall hedges and felt happy when he saw his house. The garage door was open, so he went through the garage and into the house.

"Who's there?" he heard his mother scream from upstairs.

"Me."

He heard her rush down the stairs, hurrying through the kitchen and into the den, where he stood.

"Sweetheart, what are you doing here?"

"Uh, they're not having school today."

"What?"

"Nope. They called it off."

"Where's Fitz?"

"His class stayed."

"What? What happened to your class?"

"Uh, Mrs. Jones didn't show up."

"She didn't? Well, didn't they have a substitute?"

"I don't know. There was a man who came into the class and told us to go back home. Mrs. Jones will be back tomorrow."

"Well, that's bizarre. You know, it's so bizarre I'm going to have to go up there and see what's going on."

"OK."

"Come on, you're going too."

"Why?"

"Because. I can't leave you home alone."

"Can't we just go tomorrow?"

"No. I want to see what's going on. Let's go."

"Why do I have to go to school, anyway? Can't I just stay here with you?"

"No, honey. They'll put your father and me in jail if you don't go to school. You wouldn't want that, would you?"

"No."

"Come on." She took his hand. "Let's go back up to school."

He tried to hold the lunchbox in one hand, but the lid fell open and everything dropped onto the floor.

"What happened to your lunchbox?" she asked.

"It got bent and now it won't close."

His mother put Nate's lunch into a brown paper bag and handed it to him.

They took the same path back up to the school. It was pleasant walking the streets in the morning, holding his mother's hand. But when Nate saw the stop sign and the back of the school he began to cry.

"Honey, it's OK."

"I don't want to go to school."

"You'll do just fine."

It was a hard, uncontrollable cry. His mother knelt down and cupped his head. She let him get it all out, then wiped his damp cheeks.

"Will you do me a favor?"

He nodded.

"Will you be strong for Mommy?"

There was no response.

"This is hard on me, too, sweetheart. I'm not nearly as strong as you. You're breaking my heart right now. But every little boy and girl must go to school. Fitz has to. I had to. Your father had to. Please, honey, as a favor to me. To make it easier on me. Will you please be strong? Be strong for Mommy and remember you're only there for a short time each day. Before you know it, you and Fitz will be back home playing."

Nate had stopped crying. His mother took his hand and walked up to the stop sign. The policeman had left, so they crossed on their own and walked into the school.

When they reached Mrs. Jones' classroom, Nate's mother peered in and saw his teacher standing at the front of the class reading the names from her list. She turned to Nate.

"Now, go on in there, honey."

Nate hesitated.

"Please be strong for me."

Nate walked in. He was biting his lip. He did not look around at his mother. Instead, he walked up to Mrs. Jones and told her his name.

"Well, we've been waiting for you, Mr. Jackson. Have a seat there." She pointed to a seat in the front row.

Mrs. Jones looked back at the doorway to where Nate's mother stood. Her eyes were squinting and tears streamed down her cheeks. She had both hands over her mouth and she was starting to choke.

"Oh, for heaven's sake," Mrs. Jones said. She rushed over to Nate's mother, backing her into the hall.

Nate sat down at the desk she had indicated and stared at the black-and-white tiled floor. Someone giggled. Then there was a laugh. He didn't turn around. He didn't want to look at anyone, and he tried to block out the noise. He was trying very hard to be strong.

Chapter IV

Summer has always meant sleeping in shorts with the covers off and feeling the air come in through the open window.

As boys, my two older brothers and I used to lie awake in our upstairs bedroom, sweating from the August humidity. We didn't have air conditioning in the house back then, although we did have a fan in the room. Our beds were arranged in such a way that the only equitable position for the fan was to place it where no one could feel it.

Some nights the heat became so oppressive that even Dad couldn't stand it. He would walk heavily into our room, brushing past my bed on the way to the window between my brothers' beds. He would raise the window as high as it would go. The window would crack and creak from age and lack of use.

He did this to help circulate the air upstairs. The window in my parents' room, which was down the hall from ours, would also be raised higher, and Dad would leave the doors to the two bedrooms open all night. After a while, we began to feel a slight breeze moving through the house.

I liked feeling the breeze then, but now I prefer the thought of my dad walking into our room in the middle of the night to raise the window. He was taking care of his family.

BOYS AND GIRLS

Two girls stopped Nate at the classroom door before first bell and asked if he was going to Tina's birthday party that night. They said Tina wanted to know. It was the first time these girls had ever spoken to him. Jacinta and Laura were their names.

When he answered that he would be there, Jacinta turned to Laura and said, "He's wrapped."

Laura agreed, and in an instant they were down the hall and had disappeared into another classroom. His conversations with girls always lasted about that long.

You can't talk to girls, he thought. *Girls don't know how to talk. They don't know nothing about it.* If they had stuck around he would have told them that no one would ever have him wrapped around their finger. Not even Tina.

Girls frustrated him with their judgments and rulings. He wasn't sure where he stood with them. He wasn't sure of their role in his life. They were nice to look at, though.

He liked looking at Tina. Seeing her was always the best part of the day. He would spot her white-blonde hair as she waited in line with her class against the wall outside the cafeteria. Or she would be walking with her class at the other end of the hallway and he would stop to look over at her. It made him happy. After she was gone, he would feel let down, knowing that he might not see her again until the next day.

He never mentioned Tina to anyone. None of the boys talked about girls much, and none of them had said anything about Tina's party. He wondered how many boys would be there. He could find out at lunch.

When his class reached the cafeteria, an arm-wrestling contest was going on. The winner slammed the loser's knuckles violently onto the table, and the loser got mad and slapped the winner's face.

Both knocked their chairs back when they stood up, and all of the boys rushed over to watch. The girls scrambled out of the cafeteria, screaming. Nate was disappointed when Mr. Brinker broke it up just as it was about to get good. For the rest of their break, Nate and the others argued over who would have won in a fight.

Nate forgot to ask about Tina's party with all the commotion going on, but he remembered when he walked outside for recess. He found most of the boys on the blacktop playing kickball. A game had already begun, so he was picked up by the team that was outnumbered.

All of his attention turned to the game. He wanted to do well for the team that had been forced into taking him. He wanted the captain of the team to feel that he was a good addition.

After school, Nate still didn't know which boys were going to Tina's party. He went out and stood before the row of school buses and looked at the students lined up at each one. He started at the far left bus and spied each person in line, then moved to the next bus and the next line, searching for anyone who might have been invited. Only the older kids were boarding, so Nate realized he would have to wait until later that night to see who showed up.

Nate was the only kid in his grade who walked to school. He always thought how great it must be to ride a school bus, while those on the bus told him how lucky he was that he got to walk home.

He would have liked the walk better if someone had been with him. Someone to climb the tall elm; the one with the branches that reached out over Fourth Street. Someone to jump Mrs. Crutcher's fence just to watch her get spitting mad. She was always outside in the yard after school in her dirty, worn-out housecoat and pink slippers. She always watched Nate to see if he was going to do something to her flowers. Sometimes he would pluck a petal just to hear her scream. The walk would have been a lot better with a friend.

He wondered who would be going to Tina's party, and he decided Jeff and Jerry would certainly be there. All the girls loved Jeff, and Jeff didn't go anywhere without Jerry.

When he got home he dug through the dresser for his favorite tube socks; the ones with the two red stripes. He found his blue painter trousers with the white paint blotches down the legs and the gray T-shirt with the pocket at the front. They were neatly folded in the dresser, ready for him to wear.

This would be the first time he had gone anywhere at night without his parents. When the invitation came in the mail, his mother had taken it upon herself to call Tina's house to inquire about the party, and to ask about chaperones. Every time she took action like that, Nate felt resentful. Chaperones were for little kids. She always embarrassed him like that.

Nate noticed that his mother had put Tina's birthday present on top of his toy chest. She had knocked over his G.I. Joe to make room for the present. He tossed the present onto the bed and stood the G.I. Joe back up. She must have wrapped it and put it there while he was at school.

Seeing the present reminded him of the time his mother had bought Jeff a stamp collection starter set for his birthday, when all the other boys had bought him rock albums and posters of rock stars.

After he had dressed, Nate tucked the present under his arm and went downstairs. Maybe she would be better at picking out a present for a girl. He put the present on the kitchen table. His mother, standing with her back to him in the kitchen, turned around when he walked up.

"You're not wearing that," she said.

"I want to. Please?"

She shook her head as though she were disgusted, then relented. In her opinion, boys should dress like gentlemen, not ragamuffins.

"Want to know what I bought Tina?" she asked cheerfully.

"What?"

"The prettiest little hair bows. They come in all colors."

"That'll be OK, won't it?" Nate asked.

"Oh, Tina will love them."

"Girls like that stuff, don't they?"

"Oh, my, yes."

Later on, his parents drove him to Tina's house, which was west of the school on a rundown street in a rough area. All the houses were small and old, and badly needed paint. The yards were ragged and spotty; the sidewalk chipped and broken. The front porches were warped, and some had concrete blocks for steps. Tina's house was no different. His mother voiced concern about leaving her son alone on such a street.

His father tried to calm her down, but she persisted.

"Son?" his father said. "How do you feel about it? Are you worried about ... about ..." He turned around to look at Nate in the back seat.

"About what?" Nate asked.

"About being left alone? In this neighborhood?"

"No."

"Would you like us to sit here and wait in the car?"

"No, please don't. Please go back home."

"Well, if you don't like the looks of things inside and you feel uncomfortable or threatened or anything, you call us, OK?"

"Oh, mercy!" his mother interjected. "How's he going to use the phone when he's locked up in a closet?"

"No one's going to lock me up in a closet."

She turned around to face him. "You button it!"

His father took over. "You said you spoke to the girl's mother," he said.

"Yes, but she could've told me anything. How could I really trust her? We don't even know them."

"Dad!"

"Son, go on up to the house. We'll watch you go in."

His dad was the best. He was almost always on Nate's side.

Nate hopped onto the front porch with the present under his arm. He heard his mother say from inside the car, "Well, he's dressed for this neighborhood."

Tina's mother opened the door and waved to Nate's parents in the car. She told Nate to come in, thanked him for his gift and took it into the kitchen. Nate stopped just inside the door. He couldn't believe how many girls were in the front room. Two were squeezed into the recliner, every inch of the sofa was taken up and more were sprawled out on the floor.

Most were familiar faces: Jacinta, Melissa, Patricia and Laura; Angie and Jennie, Susan and Darla. He had never seen the three girls who were sitting on the floor. Four more girls – Debbie, Tracey, Karen and Sharon – came out of the kitchen. There were no other boys. All the girls smiled politely or waved to him.

"Where's Tina?" Nate asked Tina's mother, who was standing in the entrance between the front room and the kitchen.

"She's in her room. Been there since she came home from school."

Nate heard the tapping of small footsteps coming from the hall. Everyone fell quiet and one girl on the floor reached over to turn down the volume on the TV. The tapping sounded closer, then stopped. Tina poked her head around the corner and ducked back. The girls giggled. She walked into the room, headed over to her mother and leaned back into her to examine the landscape.

Tina's mother put her arms around her. Tina waved and said hello to all the girls. When she saw Nate by the door she stepped over to him carefully and gave him a gentle hug, barely touching him, and said, "Hi Nate."

His face grew warm. "Happy birthday, Tina," he said in a shaky voice. He looked down at the floor and then up at Tina's mother, who winked at him.

Tina walked over to the sofa and squeezed herself in. He was relieved when she went away. Now that she was over there, he was able to look at her more closely. She looked different. Her hair was so curly it looked like Shirley Temple's. She wore a pink flowery dress that exposed her little knock knees. She was wearing makeup and lipstick, and there was glitter on her cheeks.

Only old women at church wear makeup and lipstick, he thought. The other girls were wearing what they normally wore to school. Tina looked as if she were going to a dance.

Nate did not like the fact that he was the only boy.

"Where are all the guys, Tina?" he asked. "I thought Jeff and Jerry were coming."

"They told me today they were," Tina said. "Oh well, who needs them?"

Tina's mother went into the kitchen. She yelled, "We'll be in here if you need anything. We'll open presents and have cake and ice cream in a bit."

A man stuck his head out of the kitchen. He had just started growing a beard and was wearing a white tank top undershirt. His straight, dark hair hung to his shoulders, and his armpit hair was exposed. He looked mean, like a pirate or a rock singer. Tina's mother pulled him back.

"Who was that?" one of the girls asked.

"That's my mom's idiot boyfriend." Tina went over and clicked off the

TV. She pulled down a small radio that was on a bookshelf above the TV and returned to her seat.

"Come on over and sit down, Nate," she said.

He sat down on the floor on the side of the recliner that was farthest from the group. He wished he had known no other guys were coming.

Tina announced to the girls: "If no other boys show up, Nate will have to do it by himself."

"What do you mean?" he asked.

"We're having a kissing contest and you're going to be the judge."

He couldn't believe it. *Does that mean …? Yes, I guess it does.* He had only kissed two girls his entire life. The way things looked he would soon be kissing a dozen. All in the same night. He scanned the room and thought about what it would be like to kiss each girl. He didn't mind going through a few ugly ones to get to the cute ones.

While they waited, the radio played and the girls screamed so hard their faces turned red. Nate had no idea what it was all about. The girls would just be looking at each other and, for no discernible reason, would break out into a scream or a burst of laughter. He fooled with his watch, and then looked up and smiled a few times so no one could tell how uncomfortable it was to be the only boy at an all-girl party. After about forty minutes, no other boys had shown up.

"Looks like you're it," Tina said. She stood up and approached Nate. She grabbed Nate's hand and pulled him up, then motioned to the girls in the recliner to get out so he could sit in what she called 'the judge's box.'

Following Tina's instructions, the girls lined up one behind the other. "Now, Nate, you have to keep your eyes closed. Each girl will call out her number, then give you a kiss for as long as she likes. After he's kissed us all he'll tell us which number was the best."

Nate started shaking inside. He really didn't know how to kiss.

One of the girls he didn't know called out the first number. She leaned over in front of him. He felt her face close. Then came a peck on the lips. It was a nice kiss; her lips were soft. The rest of the girls followed with short, soft kisses. *This is easy enough*, he thought. *Can't mess up a little peck.* He squinted to see how soon Tina would be up.

When Tina's turn came, she sat with him in the judge's box, put her arms around him and pulled him toward her. She put her lips on his and then opened her mouth. When he felt her tongue wiggle on his lips, he jerked back. He had never felt that before. He had heard about it, but he had never experienced it. He liked it, but it startled him. Tina fell onto the floor laughing, and the other girls screamed with delight.

The taste of Tina's strawberry lipstick was still on his lips. He wiped it off and the girls giggled as they watched him operate with his eyes closed.

There were three girls left to kiss after Tina. They did it like the others. Nice, short, soft kisses. Pecks.

The girls gathered around the judge's box, looking down at Nate.

"You can open your eyes," Tina said. Nate blinked repeatedly. "OK, what number was the best kisser?"

"It was you, Tina," Nate said, immediately realizing his error.

All the girls screamed, "You cheated! You looked!"

"Keep it down in there!" Tina's mother yelled from the kitchen.

The girls demanded another round and suggested using a blindfold. Tina ran to her room and brought out a red handkerchief. Before the second round began, Tina's mother poked her head into the room and saw the girls lining up in front of a blindfolded Nate.

"That does it," Tina's mother said, stomping into the room. "Tina, take that hanky off his face. Now!"

"Mom, you said you'd leave us alone."

"Your games always get out of hand. You're frightening the poor boy to death. You should've invited more boys for him to play with."

The party moved into the kitchen, where Tina opened her presents. She got a lot of clothes and seemed to like the hair bows just fine. Nate was relieved. Tina's mother cleared the table for the cake and ice cream. Nate wanted everyone to hurry up and finish so they could get on with the second round of the contest.

Tina gathered all her presents, and she and the girls returned to the front room. Nate heard Tina say something about trying on her new clothes to show the girls. He wondered if that meant the kissing contest was over. He had just decided to tag along when Tina's mother called for him to follow her. They went through the kitchen and into a hallway that led to a back bedroom. The boyfriend was in there lying on the bed, watching the small TV on the dresser.

"Why you bringing him in here?" the boyfriend asked.

"He's the only boy out there."

"So, hell?"

"The girls are scaring him to death."

"Oh, you've got to be shitting me," he said. "Hell, if I was his age …"

"You talk big now," Tina's mother said, leading Nate over to the bed.

The boyfriend looked at Nate suspiciously. Nate turned his attention to the ballgame on TV. "The Reds and Pirates," Nate said.

"You probably don't like baseball, either," he said.

"I love it. I forgot the playoffs started tonight."

Tina's mother walked out. Nate heard her yell for the girls to get their sleeping bags set up. It was eight-thirty.

Nate went over to stand at the end of the bed to get a better view of the game.

"You didn't like being in there with all them girls?"

"Sure, it was all right. They had a kissing contest and I was the judge."

"You kissed all them girls?"

Nate nodded.

"Damn, they must think you're the cat's pajamas."

"No," Nate said. "I was just the only one who could be the judge."

"Well, yeah. But Judy said you was scared."

"Nah."

"Wanna sneak back in?"

"Nah, I don't think they're gonna have the contest anymore."

"Sumbitch. I bet there's a dozen girls in there."

"Sixteen."

"Sixteen! Tell me all about this contest."

"It was great. Except they made me shut my eyes. The only way I knew a girl was close was when I felt her breath on me. It always stunk, too. It was better when I squinted. If you can see who you're kissing you don't think about their breath."

"Is that right? Well, I'll try to remember that. Sixteen girls," the boyfriend repeated. "That might be a record."

Nate hadn't thought of that.

The ballgame was tied in the fifth inning. The boyfriend caught him up on how the runs were scored. They talked about the Reds and Pirates, and who would win the pennant. They both pulled for the Reds. He was glad Tina's mother had brought him in there. Next to the kissing contest, the best part of the night was watching baseball in the back room. *With girls, everything has to be embarrassing and uncomfortable,* Nate thought. *All you can do is look at them, the cute ones, and kiss them. After that, there's nothing else to do.*

Nate heard the doorbell. He said goodbye to the boyfriend and made his way to the front of the house. As he was carefully stepping over the girls in their sleeping bags, they sang out, "Goodbye Nate," and it came out in a tune.

He saw his mother at the door with a smile so big her gums and long teeth were showing. He would never hear the end of it. He was sure his mother would tell the story over and over at church while he was present.

He wished his dad had come to the door instead. He would have kidded Nate about the girls singing out like that, but he would have kept the joke between them.

Chapter V

Grandma Snyder begged her two grandsons to help old Mrs. Cavanaugh with a school project for her special-needs class.

"What does she want us to do?" Nate asked.

"Drive to Manson's Market and try to persuade her students to get into your car," Grandma Snyder said. "She's teaching them about strangers."

"That's creepy," Fitz said. "We'll get arrested."

"No, no," she said. "Mrs. Cavanaugh has talked to the store manager. He's agreed to let them practice out in the parking lot. She wants to test her students in a real-life environment. Nate, you'll help sweet Mrs. Cavanaugh, won't you? She's awfully fond of you boys."

"I've got basketball practice after school," Nate said. "I won't be home till 5:30."

"Fitz, dear, Mrs. Cavanaugh used to babysit you. Can't you help her after school tomorrow?"

"Oh, all right," Fitz said.

After school the next day, Fitz drove to Manson's Market and parked. Mrs. Cavanaugh approached him as he was getting out.

"Get back in your car and drive to the front of the store," she said. "I'll send one of the students out. Now, be persuasive. Tell them you'll drive them home or take them for ice cream. Thank you, sweet lamb, for doing this."

Fitz pulled his car around to the front of the store, and out came a black girl with the body of an overweight adult and the face of a child. Fitz motioned the girl toward the open window on the passenger's side.

"Hi there," Fitz smiled. "What's your name?"

"No."

"I'm Fitz. Would you like a lift home?"

"What? No! What?"

"I can drive you home. On the way we can stop for ice cream. Would you like that?"

"No. Huh?"

A neighbor, Mrs. Malandain, stopped in front of Fitz's car. She looked at Fitz, and then at the girl, and then back at Fitz.

Fitz could not persuade the girl to get into his car, so he drove off. He hoped his part of the project was done, so he went home.

About an hour later, Mrs. Cavanaugh's car pulled up at Grandma Snyder's house. Fitz walked two doors down to his grandma's as soon as he saw the car.

Mrs. Cavanaugh appeared upset. "Well, Mrs. Malandain complained to the assistant manager that Nate Jackson was outside trying to molest girls. The assistant manager called the police because he didn't know about the school project. The store manager and I talked to the police and straightened it out, but Mrs. Malandain wasn't convinced.

"She went around the store telling everyone Nate Jackson was outside molesting little girls. I told her it was Fitz, not Nate. And that Fitz was working on behalf of the school to help prevent our special needs students from getting into cars with strangers. She wouldn't hear of it and left in a huff."

"Well, as long as Mrs. Malandain thinks it was Nate, I'm OK with that," Fitz joked.

The next week, Mrs. Cavanaugh and the school principal paid a visit to the Malandains' house. It turned out Mrs. Malandain had just started losing her mind. She died a year later, convinced that Nate Jackson was molesting girls in the parking lot of Manson's Market.

Nate told anyone who would listen that he wasn't the molester; that it was Fitz. "And Fitz didn't do it," he added. But from that day forward, the town was a little wary of the Jackson boys. The general consensus was that something just wasn't quite right about them.

CONTEMPT

The judge ordered all those pleading not guilty to sit in the first two rows and those pleading guilty to come up and form a line against the wall. In the back of the courtroom, four bums stood up. One by one they squeezed past a tidy, elderly woman who was seated at the end of the row. She looked like a church organist. The bums apologized for bumping her.

"Quite all right, gentlemen," the woman said. "Pardon me."

The bums stopped at the wall and leaned against it. This irritated the court bailiff, who ordered them to stand up straight. They shoved themselves off the wall, arched their backs and stuck out their chins. One of them saluted. When the bailiff turned his back they relaxed and leaned on the wall again.

The bums had no teeth, and their pink and black gums showed when they smiled among themselves. They looked very happy to see one another in this setting.

A boy named Josh Compton sat down in the front row. He watched the first vagabond approach the podium to address the judge.

"Oh my word. I can smell you from here," said district judge Alice Singleton. She grimaced as she waved a hand repeatedly in front of her nose. The glasses she kept on a chain around her neck made a clicking noise from the motion she made with her hand. "State your name."

"Ray Gudgel," the man said, then cleared his throat.

"What do you plead to the charge of public drunkenness?"

"Guilty."

"Of course you're guilty," the judge said. "I accept your plea. Are you drunk now?"

"Oh, no, ma'am. I haven't had a drink in twenty years."

"What? Then how do you explain this charge of public drunkenness?"

"I don't try to explain it. If you say I was drunk, then I was drunk, your highness."

"What did you call me?"

"Your honor."

"You said your highness."

"Yes, ma'am. Where I come from it is used with utmost respect."

The other bums stirred a little and exchanged gummy smiles.

"Where do you come from?"

"Around Front Street. Near the depot."

The bums snickered and slapped each other on the back. The bailiff turned around and gave them a dirty look.

"You know I could lock you up for contempt?" the judge said.

"Yes, ma'am. I know. Oh yes, I know."

The judge gave him two months to pay a fine of one hundred dollars. The bailiff took his arm and escorted him out.

Seeing how the judge handled her courtroom, Josh wondered if it might be best just to plead guilty and be done with it. What judge would be sympathetic to a kid charged with running a red light? Especially this judge. She was the type who felt compelled to do all the talking. All output, no input.

However, he thought he was innocent and wanted the opportunity to tell her about it. He knew what had happened. He knew the truth. A judge would respect the truth. If only he could make her forget that he was sixteen.

He remembered everything that had happened on the night in question. He could see it in his mind's eye. He had finished work at the grocery store at nine. At the end of his shift he had watered the cabbages, celery and all the greens, then packed the produce into deep bins, shoveled ice on top and rolled them to the back, where they would be stored in the walk-in refrigerator until morning. That was his favorite part of the job.

When he left the store, the rain had suddenly started to fall in large drops. It was raining so hard he flipped the wipers to their highest setting. He was on the bypass, approaching an intersection, and the light up ahead was green. He noticed two cars stopped at the intersection on the right-hand side, one behind the other.

When he looked back at the road, the light had turned yellow. He tapped the brake and felt the car hydroplane a little. It had scared him, so he let off the brake and glided through the intersection. He had seen the reflection of the traffic light on the hood change from yellow to red.

He gripped the steering wheel with both hands. Josh had never felt a car hydroplane before. He wasn't sure he was in control of the car. He thought about slowing to a stop but was too afraid to do anything too assertively. In the rear-view mirror, the headlights of a car sped up to him and began tailgating. He hoped the car would go around him on the left. Blue lights flashed and pulsated in the mirror. It was a jolt to the senses.

He pulled over to the shoulder and stopped, then punched the seat. "Dammit! I didn't run that light! I didn't!"

A policeman's mustached face appeared at the driver's window. Rain pelted the plastic baggy covering his hat. He asked Josh if he was aware that he had run a red light.

"The light was yellow, sir," Josh said. "I tried to stop but the roads being wet and all ..."

The officer took Josh's driver's license and proof of insurance, then went back to his car. Five minutes later he returned with a citation and a court date circled.

"Be more careful, son," the officer said.

"Yes, sir." Josh watched the officer get into his cruiser, then crumpled the citation and threw it to the floor.

He leaned back, trying to get comfortable on the courtroom bench. It popped and creaked. The bench reminded him of a church pew the way it looked and in its hardness.

The judge shook her head at another bum. "How many more months can I put this off for you?" she asked. "Why can't you pay?"

The bum didn't speak. He made no effort to talk at all. He just stood there, half-smiling.

"I guess he was born without a tongue," the judge said. "Put him in jail."

All the guilty pleas were done. The only ones left in the gallery were the three pleading not guilty, and the elderly woman sitting at the back.

"Those pleading not guilty follow the assistant county prosecutor," said the judge, who stood up and exited the courtroom through a back door.

The prosecutor – a short, round woman with a boy's haircut – motioned for the two adults and Josh to follow her and the bailiff into a side room. The elderly woman remained seated. She picked up her purse and her Bible and set them in her lap.

The side room was small and consisted of a small desk with a chair on each side. The prosecutor sat down behind the desk and set her folders down on it. The bailiff stood behind her. The two adults and Josh stood over the empty chair. "OK. Josh Compton, you're first. Have a seat."

Josh sensed that the prosecutor was as impatient as the judge. She had taken on her colleague's personality.

"All right, honey, it says here you ran a red light and it was Officer Goodman who cited you."

"Yes, ma'am."

She turned around and asked the bailiff to bring Officer Goodman in.

"OK, honey. Goodman's been on the force fifteen years and has done a solid job. If I'm the judge, I'm going to trust Goodman's judgment on this one."

Officer Goodman walked in, greeted the prosecutor by placing his large hand on her shoulder, and then stood behind her. He looked at Josh. His mustache was gone.

"But ma'am, you haven't heard the story," Josh said.

"OK, honey. Go ahead."

"The light was yellow."

The prosecutor looked up from the file and waited for something more from him. When nothing came, she turned and handed the file to Officer Goodman.

"Oh yes, I remember. It was raining that night," Officer Goodman said, leafing through the file. "You ran that red light clear as day."

Josh leaned back in his chair as the prosecutor took the file back from Goodman.

"Now, if you plead guilty we'll give you the option of going to driving school and this traffic violation will be taken off your record."

"But I'm not guilty," Josh said. "Doesn't anyone care about that? The road was real wet. The car might have turned sideways if I had mashed on the brakes. And the light was still yellow when I entered the intersection."

There was a hush in the room. The prosecutor winked at the adults standing behind Josh. Josh felt even younger than he was, as if the prosecutor and the adults knew how the system worked while he did not.

"It's going to be your word, a sixteen-year-old's, against the word of a professional law enforcement officer. I don't care what you decide; I'm just giving you the odds. If you go out there and plead not guilty and lose, you will be charged court costs and you may or may not be allowed to attend traffic school. If the judge decides not to give you the traffic school option, the state will take three points off your driving record and that will leave you with nine. If you lose the other nine, the state will take away your license."

Josh shook his head and slumped down in the seat.

"Well, what's it going to be?"

"I don't know." Josh looked around him.

"We don't have all day here."

"Well, can I … can I use the bathroom?"

"It's out that way." She pointed to a door that led into a hallway.

One of the adults was going to say something to the prosecutor, but he held his tongue when he saw Josh stand up and look at him.

Josh didn't need to use the bathroom. He wanted to phone his older sister. She would know what to do. He found a payphone in the lobby, called home and waited for five rings, but there was no answer. *Now what?* he said to himself. He let it ring three more times. *The judge won't even get a chance to hear what happened, what really happened.*

He felt a hand pat his shoulder and turned around.

"Oh, hello Mr. Williams," Josh said, hanging up the phone. Mr. Williams was one of the deacons at his church. He wore a cowboy hat everywhere he went.

"Hi, son," Mr. Williams said. "What are you doing here?"

"I'm in court for running a red light."

"Oh, oh."

"Yeah. Only I'm innocent. The light was yellow. The prosecutor says I should plead guilty."

"Well, they know best. You gotta take your lumps sometimes."

"What are you doing here?" Josh asked.

"Oh, I come here every afternoon. Just killing time."

"Well, I guess I better get back."

"OK, now. Don't worry about it. I've had plenty of tickets."

Mr. Williams was a retired banker and one of the most respected men in town. He watched Josh start down the long hallway. His mind got to thinking. He had seen the young man at church the previous week and had wanted to talk to him about something. "Let's see, now. What was it?" Mr. Williams said to himself. "Wait, I got it."

"Josh!" he yelled, waving at Josh, who was halfway down the hall.

Josh turned around and started back. "Yes, sir?"

"I've been meaning to talk to you about the night I saw you driving out on the bypass."

"Yes, sir."

"I was stopped at a stoplight and saw you coming up the road. I could see the light turn yellow and you hit your brakes and then kept on through the intersection. A cop was behind me. He pulled around and zoomed off after you. I thought to myself then, 'Boy, old Josh has got it now.'"

"Yep."

"Is that why you're here now?"

"Yep."

"You didn't run that light," Mr. Williams said. "You tried to stop and you still made it to the intersection while the light was yellow. I thought at the time the cop was being awful picky. I was hoping he'd let you off with a warning."

"He didn't."

"Well, I don't think you should be ticketed for that. You'd be a fool to plead guilty."

"They're giving me no other choice. The prosecutor said it's my word against the officer's."

"Well, I'll testify for you," he said. "Use me. I'll help you."

"Really?"

"Sure. What courtroom you in?"

"C."

"I'm on my way."

Josh ran down the hall and opened the door to the small room. One of the adults got up from the chair and went into the courtroom. Josh plopped down into the chair, grinning.

"I'm pleading not guilty," he said, looking back and forth between the prosecutor and Officer Goodman. "I've got a witness."

"What witness?" she asked.

"He's on his way to the courtroom right now."

"Where was he when you ran the stoplight?"

"I didn't run the stoplight. My witness was at the intersection in front of the officer. He saw everything. I just ran into him in the lobby. What luck, huh?"

The prosecutor frowned at Officer Goodman, who shook his head at her.

"Do you remember a car being in front of you at the intersection?" she asked Officer Goodman.

"Heck, I don't know. Maybe."

She turned to Josh. "If you want to plead not guilty, I can't stop you. I can only warn you of the consequences."

"Am I going to win?"

"No. Now get up. James Partin, you're next. Take a seat here. Josh, you stand over there. Not there. *There.*"

The two adults were persuaded to plead guilty. Court reconvened with the judge imposing a fine on them and they were dismissed. Josh came up and sat alone at one of the tables. The prosecutor sat at another.

Mr. Williams took off his cowboy hat and sat behind Josh in the gallery. The elderly woman was still at the back of the room. She kept one hand on the Bible and crossed herself several times with the other.

"Only one not pleading guilty, eh?" the judge said to the prosecutor and winked. "OK, let's get this over with. Bailiff, bring in Officer Goodman."

Officer Goodman took a seat in the box that was usually reserved for the jury. Looking into the gallery, the judge spotted the form of an old man sitting in the front row behind Josh. She brought her glasses up to her eyes and took a long look at the old man. Mr. Williams waved at her. She said to herself, "It's old man Williams. That old SOB."

"You, there, in the gallery. What business do you have with this court?" the judge asked, pretending not to know who he was.

Mr. Williams stood up, buttoned his coat and said, "Your honor, I'm here as a witness for Josh Compton."

"Well, you can sit down for now," the judge said. She opened a file and began reading the police report.

"OK, Mr. Compton, step up to the podium. The police officer says you ran a red light. Are you saying you did not?" The judge's head was down, her eyes fixed on the file.

"That's right, your honor. I did not run a red light."

"Officer Goodman, step to the podium," the judge said. "You may be seated for now, Mr. Compton."

Officer Goodman walked long-legged in front of the judge's bench, a black gun attached to his hip. The leather holster cracked with each step.

"What happened?" the judge asked, closing the file.

"On the night in question, I was stopped at a stoplight headed westbound and saw the boy's car approaching the intersection headed north. The light changed to red and he ran right through it."

The judge nodded at the officer. "You may be seated. Mr. Compton, come back to the podium."

"So, what's your version? And leave out the 'you knows' and 'like this' and 'like that,' and all that other juvenile nonsense. Just give it to me straight and make it as concise as possible. Let's not make it an all-day affair. OK?"

Josh was afraid to speak. He trembled. "The light was yellow when I drove up and the light was ahead of me a ways and up ahead was the intersection, and also it was raining and, and then," he stammered. "I'm sorry, your honor, I'm nervous. I've never done this before. I don't want you to yell at me. I'll be quick."

The judge rolled her eyes and signaled for him to continue.

"I tried to stop a ways back when I saw the light change to yellow, but I began hydroplaning so I just went on through. I was afraid I'd lose control of the car if I pressed too hard on the brake."

"How fast were you going?"

"About fifty."

"Is that right, Officer Goodman? You can answer from your seat."

"Yes, your honor. That was his speed."

"Did Mr. Compton try to stop?"

"No, your honor. He went right through the red light without hesitating."

"Were the roads in a condition that would have made it hazardous to stop?" the judge asked.

"No, your honor."

"I don't see any reason for this to go any further. Do you, Mr. Compton?"

"Yes, your honor. I have a witness to back up my story."

"Oh, yes. You may be seated, Mr. Compton."

She eyed Mr. Williams. "You, there. Step up to the podium and state your name."

Mr. Williams sprang to his feet and hustled up to the front. "I'm Russell Williams, your honor."

"Mr. Compton, you may question your witness. You may remain seated if you'd like."

"Thank you, your honor," Josh said. He was gaining confidence. "Mr. Williams, please tell the court where you were and what you saw."

"That was real good, son. Sounded real professional," Mr. Williams said.

"Just tell us what you think you saw so we can get this over with," the judge snapped.

"Just as Josh said, I was in my car headed westbound and was stopped at the stoplight in front of the police officer. I saw Josh's car stand up in the back, the way cars do when the brakes are applied. He hit the brake as soon as the light turned yellow. Then he let it off and went through the intersection. But the light didn't turn red until he was in the intersection."

"Anything else?" the judge said.

"Well, it was raining hard and the roads were wet and slick as ice."

"Anything else?" the judge looked at Josh.

"No, your honor," Josh said.

"Well, now, also your honor, if I may, I can vouch for Josh's character. He attends church regularly and the preacher calls on him to read Bible verses on Sunday nights."

"That's enough, Williams. Be seated."

Mr. Williams gave the judge a sour look and turned away from the podium. He bent down to Josh and whispered, "Don't look good, son. She's as mean as a snake. Just like her old man." Mr. Williams sat down in the gallery and waited for the verdict.

"Josh Compton, stand up," the judge said. "I find you guilty. I trust Officer Goodman's judgment over seven hundred and seventy-seven witnesses. The fine is sixty-seven dollars and fifty cents plus court costs, which makes it one-hundred and five dollars to be paid in full in three weeks."

The judge turned to the prosecutor: "Do we want to give him the option of driving school so he can have this taken off his record?"

"Yes, your honor."

"Well, Mr. Compton, I'm going to give you the option to enroll in driving school. Look at me. It will be good for you and it will erase this from your record. But most importantly, it will make you more knowledgeable about driver safety. It will teach you to be a defensive driver. Hey, you. Look at me when I'm talking."

Josh stared down at the hardwood tabletop. He made a fist. *She didn't listen*, he thought. *Her mind was made up from the start. She don't care about the truth.* He clenched and unclenched his fist, then struck the table with a heavy blow. It sounded like a clap of thunder. The judge and assistant prosecutor jumped.

"Don't you pitch a fit in front of me, you little hothead," the judge said. "Now get out of here and don't let me see you again."

Josh could have strangled her. Then suddenly it all went out of him and he felt alone. He stood up and tucked the chair under the table.

Mr. Williams put his hat on and patted Josh's shoulder. They walked together toward the exit. "The deck was stacked against you, son. I knew it was trouble when I saw who the judge was."

"Why?"

"Well, I'll tell you. Come on outside. There's a story behind her verdict. I'm afraid it's all my fault we lost ... Why, hello there, Mrs. Singleton." Mr. Williams blushed. He tipped his hat to the elderly woman in the back. "I didn't see you there. This is the judge's mother, Josh."

She nodded at Mr. Williams, then peered into Josh's face.

"Do not despair, young man," she said. "Do you hear? Do not despair."

"Yes, ma'am. Thank you." Josh bowed slightly.

Mr. Williams opened the door for Josh. He looked back to make sure Mrs. Singleton wasn't following them out. When he had closed the door behind him, Mr. Williams said to Josh, "You've just learned a valuable lesson about how this world works. Come on, I'll tell you."

Still seated, Mrs. Singleton crossed herself several times, then bowed her head and began to pray. "Dear Lord, please change Alice's heart. She used to be such a sweet little girl. She used to love all of her classmates, and all of the dogs and cats on our street, and the birds and squirrels, and every living thing. Now I don't think she loves or cares for anything anymore. Maybe one of these days when she sees me sitting here it will remind her of her childhood and all the good and wonderful things in life. I will stay seated here for as long as it takes. Please, Lord, enter her heart and don't ever leave. In Jesus' name, amen."

Chapter VI

During the warm months, Kandt worked the night shift at the newspaper so he could have his days free. There were so many things he liked to do outside when the sun was up. Golf was his favorite. The best part to him was climbing the hills, feeling the turf underfoot and the weight of the golf bag on his shoulders. Afterward, he would be tired and sweaty, and it was pleasant to sit in the shade of the trees at the back of his apartment and feel the breeze when there was one.

When the weather turned cold, he would go to the newsroom supervisor and take whatever day job was available. The day job required that he walk to the various courthouses downtown to pick up public records. By November, he was ready to put his golf clubs away and start wearing long-sleeved shirts and a heavy coat and boots to walk the cold, damp, leaf-sodden streets of Lexington.

This schedule seemed perfectly natural to him until one night, as summer drew to a close, when he found himself in bed and unable to sleep. He realized how disappointed he was with himself. He held various low-level jobs at the newspaper; he did not make a lot of money; he did not have a girlfriend and rarely brought a woman back to his apartment. He wanted a girlfriend, but he wasn't going to force it. It wasn't the kind of thing he could push. It had to come naturally. He wasn't sure where he was going in life or what he was doing.

He would have liked to make more money, but he wasn't going to jump into something just because it paid better. He wanted work that had meaning; something of real consequence. Like the time when he was a teen and Mr. McMurtry, his neighbor, had died. His mother asked him to mow the lawn for the widow McMurtry. He mowed it all that spring and summer before he left for college.

Mowing the yard meant a great deal to Mrs. McMurtry because her hus-

band had taken great pride in his yard, and Kandt had kept it up just as nice. Whenever she tried to pay him he refused, and she would start to cry and tell him how grateful she was. He always told her to think nothing of it. He would like to feel that way about work again. Dreaming of that kind of work settled his nerves to the point that he could relax and go to sleep.

On the nights he couldn't sleep, he would lie in bed and ask himself if he was happy. He thought about all he did and all the places he went in a day, in a month, in a season and throughout the year. From April to November, he got up early to fish or play golf. He played golf two or three times a week. To take a break from golf, he would fish. But golf was his main concern. He was a pretty good player and there was always the belief that he was getting better and was very close to a breakthrough.

After fishing or playing golf, he would return to his apartment, and if no one was in the pool he would swim laps to burn whatever energy he had left. Then he would pour beer into a frosted stein, sit in the shade on the patio and look into the backyard of the house that was behind the apartment.

A swing set stood in the yard, and a tire hung from a tree. The yard was usually empty. He liked it better when the kids were home playing in the yard. Birds trilling put him in the mood to lie down. He usually had an hour to kill before he had to leave for work.

He worked in the sports department, compiling horse racing entries and results, and baseball box scores from all the major league games. The copy came to him rough. He cleaned it up so that it was neat and easy to read in the next morning's paper. He enjoyed the work even though it was tedious.

After the shift he would stop at Caddyshack's. It would be closed, but he knew the bartender and she would let him in. He was allowed to go behind the bar and pour his own stein while she washed down the counters, stacked chairs on top of tables, counted the money and turned out the lights. He served as her lookout while she smoked in the walk-in freezer.

She was a good, efficient worker who wiped the bar so clean that the light from outside shone on it clearly afterward. He enjoyed sitting there drinking, watching her tidy up and complain about that night's customers, or her crazy sister or no-account husband.

That was how he spent the spring, summer and early fall. When he switched to a day shift for the winter, he spent most of his time walking downtown to *record bankruptcies, divorces, civil suits, and felony and misdemeanor arrests. While walking the streets in the oldest part of the city, he tried to imagine what it must have been like to live there in the old days. Lunch was taken at one of the many dives, hanging out with the old-timers.*

Winter forced everyone inside, and the only good game inside was basketball. He played in two leagues: one at Nicholasville Elementary and the other at Beaumont Middle. Kandt was a key member of both teams. He had never won a championship, although both teams had championship potential.

When he had gone through everything his life consisted of, he decided he was happy after all. There wasn't anything he regretted, and he never once dreaded getting out of bed in the morning. He did wonder what he could do about the times when he felt bad about himself. Sometimes he would finish swimming laps at the pool and would be toweling off when a big group would come through the gate and arrange the pool chairs close together, moving a table with an umbrella toward them.

Usually it was three guys and three girls. They always brought a cooler and they would mix drinks on the table. The girls would be pretty and they would all toast each other. The guys would say something and the girls would cackle with laughter. He wished they would invite him over, but there was no reason for them to do so. Everyone was matched up. He was unnecessary.

It struck him then that he was alone in the world. He would look over at the group and spot one of them looking at him, before quickly looking away. It gave him the impression that they thought ill of him for always being alone.

In the newsroom there was always a lot of ambition on display. He was the same age as or older than many of the managers and assistant editors. Whenever he needed to see one of them about something, they acted irritated by the interruption, as though he were taking up their important time with his piddling, insignificant business. His presence seemed to be an insult to their ambition because he didn't strive to be more than he was.

It was now late fall, and Kandt had been notified by the newsroom supervisor that he could start working days the week after Thanksgiving. That was satisfactory. He tried not to worry about anything. The cold weather was coming on and he was looking forward to sloshing downtown in the wet gloom of midday to think more about his situation and whether he could continue to live the way he was living.

THE ANARCHIST

The Wednesday before Thanksgiving, there was a message on Kandt's phone from his old friend King, who said he would be in Wilmore for the holiday weekend. The message said that the rest of their old gang would also be in town and that the plan was to meet at Kandt's apartment on Friday, and to go from there to play basketball at the YMCA.

Kandt felt like doing somersaults across the room. He hadn't seen his old buddies in years. And they were all coming over to his place. They would pile into his apartment and have a grand time. There had never been more than one or two people in his apartment. Now there would be five. He went into the kitchen, pulled down a bottle of whiskey and toasted himself and his friends.

At eleven o'clock on Friday morning, there was a knock at Kandt's door. He opened it and smiled at the sight of four familiar faces. The faces were fatter, and there was some facial hair, but the eyes still belonged to the boys he grew up with. There was vigorous handshaking all around and a hug from King. Kandt pulled all the boys inside and asked them to sit down. The sofa and love seat filled up quickly, so Kandt grabbed a chair from the kitchen and brought it over.

On the sofa sat Big Jim, wearing a beard to cover his newly fat face. Sitting next to him was Tree Stump Brian, who was short but as thick as a sycamore. As a kid, Tree Stump Brian was always looking for a fight. In the love seat were Slight Jeff, who had rounded out a little and had grown a goatee to help darken his baby face, and King the Exuberant. King hadn't changed a bit. His neat, trim physique matched his optimistic outlook on life. He never let anything weigh him down.

"Man, it's good to see you guys again," Kandt said. "You have no idea. We got out of school and everyone scattered like bird shot. Where's everyone living now? Wait a second, let me get my address book."

Kandt wrote that King was living just outside Minneapolis, Big Jim in Chicago, Tree Stump Brian in Miami and Slight Jeff in Atlanta. After he wrote down their addresses and phone numbers, he looked around the room. Everything was strangely quiet. Everyone seemed to want to say something, but for some reason they were holding back.

Lately, Kandt had found himself growing uncomfortable whenever a conversation extended beyond polite exchanges. Work would most likely be the next topic, and he wanted to avoid that subject. He did not have much of a job and he was OK with that, but his lack of initiative seemed to bother everyone else.

Looking at all the high tops on the floor, he said, "Should we go play ball?"

King spoke up. "Wait, we just got here. Don't you want to know what everyone's been up to?"

"Oh, I don't know," Kandt said. "I'm just glad you're all well and sitting here in my apartment."

"Do you even know what I *do*?" King asked.

"Sell cars, don't you?"

"Sell cars," King said in disgust. "See, you don't even know. I don't sell cars. I close the deal. I'm the business manager at the largest Chevrolet dealer in Greater Minneapolis."

"That's great," Kandt said. "Let's go play ball."

"Wait, wait," King said. "Are you still at the newspaper?"

"Yeah. In fact, I start working days next week."

"Really? Is there a future in that?"

"Yeah, until spring."

"What does that mean? What happens in the spring?"

"I go back to working nights in the sports department so I can have my days freed up."

"Why do you want your days freed up?"

"So I can fish and play golf."

"Oh," King said, confused.

"Well, let's go play ball." Kandt stood up and the others followed suit. All except King.

"Oh, sit down, we've got all day," King said.

Everyone sat back down except Kandt.

"The best players are there now," Kandt said. "If we wait any longer we'll be playing with ourselves."

"We're having a conversation here," King said. "You're my friend and I haven't seen you in years. Now sit down. I want to know what you've been up to. For instance, are you seeing anyone?"

"As a matter of fact, no. I'm not seeing anyone."

"Is that right?" King said. "Did you know that I'm still married?"

"I hadn't heard otherwise."

"All the boys are married," King said, nodding toward the others. "I was wondering," he continued, putting a finger to his lip. "Maybe you've got a good thing going, being single. You're free. You don't have to report in or put up with nagging."

"That's true," Kandt said. "But I happen to think marriage would be fine, too."

"You'd like to marry a *woman*?" King asked.

"Sure, if I met the right one."

"Well, that's a relief," King said, clapping his hands. Then he leaned back and lifted his feet in mock celebration. "Well, you never know."

The others looked at Kandt, then looked away. They seemed embarrassed by King's behavior.

Kandt could either go over and bust King's lip or stand there and take it. He chose to take it.

King began a new line of questioning. "Seems like you've lived here a long time. Do you *like* living in an apartment?"

Kandt went over and opened the front door. "Come on, let's go play ball. We can talk on the way there."

The YMCA was only three blocks away, so Kandt and the boys decided to walk.

King continued the interrogation on foot. "Do you ever get a vacation, Kandt?"

"Yeah, I usually just go fishing somewhere around here. Elkhorn Creek,

Little Hickman or Jessamine Creek."

"Jessamine Creek?" King sounded surprised. "That's where we went when we were kids."

"Yeah," Kandt said.

"If I have a good December, which I will, my boss is going to send me to Myrtle Beach," King said.

"Fantastic. They've got great golf courses there, I hear."

"Yeah, well, it's an incentive to do well. It gets people motivated."

"I don't think I'm very motivated," Kandt said. "I have absolutely no ambition. Nothing excites me."

"Ah, bull," King said. "There are salesmen who work for me who are just like you. I just give them a good kick in the ass."

"Really?"

"Yeah. You just need a good kick in the ass."

"I'm afraid I'd disappoint you. I don't like anyone telling me what to do. I like to be left alone."

"And what's it gotten you? A crummy apartment and no woman."

"I can't argue with you there."

"Well, then, reach for something big at the newspaper. Sure, you'll have to take orders for a time, but before you know it you'll be the one giving the orders."

King awaited Kandt's rebuttal but when it didn't come he said, "It's settled then. Now, let's play ball."

The inquisition was over.

At the gym they had to wait for a game to end before they could take the court. They played the winners of the previous game. They won their first game with Kandt, Tree Stump Brian and Big Jim scoring all the points.

The three remembered to keep the ball away from King and Slight Jeff. They had always talked a big game, even when they were little, but once the game started there was a tacit understanding among the others about whom the ball should go to. King and Slight Jeff had no talent for basketball or any other sport. They just didn't know it.

After the game, the losing team picked up their things to leave. There was no one waiting on the sideline for the winners. A commotion outside the gym door signaled that more players were about to arrive.

When the door opened they could hear a man say, harshly, "Hey! Shut that mouth! You talk when I tell you to talk!"

Shoved from behind, a boy stumbled into the gym. He was followed by a tall, bald-headed man who looked out of place in a sweatshirt and shorts. He looked like a drill sergeant out of uniform. Behind the man trailed three more boys, all of whom looked to be in their early teens.

"Who has winner?" the man yelled, as if he were still talking to one of the boys.

"No one," Kandt said. He felt like adding: 'you bald-headed son of a bitch.'

"All right, then," the man said, pulling off his sweatshirt. There was no T-shirt underneath; he was going to play skins. He looked like a bear with thick, black hair covering his chest and back. "Give us a minute to warm up," he demanded.

When they were ready, the boys called out "Dad" and asked who they should guard. The man sized up the opposition and gave each son an assignment.

"Now guard them," the man said. "No half-ass."

Early in the game, the man grabbed a rebound and threw a football pass downcourt to one of his sons, who ran ahead of Tree Stump Brian to catch it. It was a perfect pass and a beautiful catch. The boy banked the ball too hard off the backboard. It didn't even touch the rim. The boy's father shouted as if he had been shot and ran to the other end of the floor to confront the boy. He stood over him for a moment, then shoved him in the chest. The boy staggered but remained on his feet. He ran back upcourt.

"Get your goddamn head out of your goddamn ass!" the man screamed.

Kandt and King had stopped to watch.

"Look at that," Kandt said.

King chuckled.

"Let me take that bald-headed MFer," Kandt said to King. "You get my man."

Kandt felt his teeth grind. He studied the man as he walked upcourt. The man had a clean, slick head and a band of black hair around back that stretched from ear to ear. His barrel chest and long, muscular arms and legs looked physically fit. He was a well-built specimen.

The man continued to shout at the son who had missed the layup. He walked the ball upcourt, dribbling high and slow, and shouted for the boy to get open.

I'll get him, Kandt thought.

Creeping up to meet the man at midcourt, Kandt wanted to do something: steal the ball, block his shot, something. The man was watching for the boy to get open. Kandt moved up and hand-checked him, pushing him a little harder than he had intended. The man glared at Kandt like he wanted to stab him, then took off for the basket. Kandt stayed with him step for step. At the foul line, the man pulled up. He head faked, but Kandt didn't leave his feet.

Seeing the ball right there before him, Kandt slapped at it. He caught most of the man's arm and a little bit of the ball. He swiped at the ball again, but this time he karate-chopped both arms. The man stopped and glared at Kandt again. He offered Kandt the ball, like he wanted him to have another go at it. Kandt went for it, but the man pulled the ball back and raised it level with Kandt's forehead, and thumped him with it twice between the eyes. The blows startled Kandt and knocked him backward.

"Hey!" Tree Stump Brian shouted, rushing over to the man. "You can't do that!"

Shaking off the two thumps, Kandt stood beside Big Jim and watched Tree Stump Brian confront the man. Everything was happening in slow motion. The man's eyes darkened with rage and his bald head turned pink. He paid no attention to Tree Stump Brian. He stared at Kandt the whole time Tree Stump Brian was yapping.

"You little piece of shit! I'll kick your goddamn ass!"

"Yeah?" Kandt said. "You're going to kick my ass?"

Kandt started toward the man. Everything was still in slow motion. The man dropped the basketball and swung at Kandt, but Kandt stepped back in time to avoid it. Kandt had an opening to throw a punch of his own, but he spotted one of the man's sons out of the corner of his eye just standing, watching.

"Do you really want to fight in front of your kids?" Kandt asked.

"I don't give a good goddamn," the man said. "You're not gonna foul me like that and get away with it."

Big Jim put his arms around Kandt and slung him away. After a short break to cool their tempers, it was decided that Big Jim would guard the man. The rest of the game was like tiptoeing through a minefield. Everyone feared the next blow-up.

Kandt and his friends won the game. They decided it would be best to leave promptly to avoid another confrontation, but two of the man's sons ran after them and asked if they would stay for a rematch. There was no one else in the gym, so if Kandt and his friends left, the man and his sons would not have a game.

The man watched his sons pleading. "Let 'em go," the man said. "They're weak."

During the walk back to the apartment, Kandt denounced the man. He had him whipped, burned and buried alive, but the others thought Kandt was overreacting.

"I should've slugged that guy," Kandt said. "But I didn't want to hit him in front of his kids. It would have hurt them to see that. I'd like to catch him alone sometime and give him a piece of my mind."

"What would you say?" King asked.

"I'd call him a tyrant."

"Oh, now," King said. "He was all right. He's old school."

"He's a tyrant," Kandt said.

"How can you say that?"

"You saw the way he treated his kids."

"He's what you call a disciplinarian."

"He's what you call a tyrant. Did you notice that none of his sons came to his defense when we were about to go at it?"

"So? That kid he yelled at was probably rooting for you."

"That's why I say he's a tyrant. If I got into a fight with your old man, you'd want to kill me. As much as me and my old man fought, I still wouldn't let some SOB start a fight with him."

King did not answer.

Kandt continued: "Pushing, shoving, ordering those kids around. He thinks he can control them. No one should have control over another human. I hope those boys get fed up one day and sock him in the jaw."

King shook his head and gave a look as if arguing with a madman was pointless. "If only you were this passionate about things that matter," he said.

Kandt did not reply. He was thinking about the tyrant.

The friends walked to their car instead of back to Kandt's apartment. Kandt invited them in for a glass of water, but they said they wanted to go. It was a rotten end to a disappointing day. Kandt apologized for the blow-up. They waved him off, saying it was nothing. Everyone wished each other luck and Kandt watched them pile into the car and drive away.

Climbing the stairs to his apartment, Kandt was troubled by all that had happened and the way his friends had left so abruptly. *So we disagree on how a father treats his sons,* he thought. *That's no big deal.*

What really bothered him was the disappointed expression King had worn all day. It was an expression he had seen on many people's faces over the years. It was obvious that King disapproved of the way Kandt conducted his life.

Kandt thought: *I respect a man who strives to be something big and important. Can't that same man respect someone who chooses to be neither?*

Chapter VII

Late in the game, Mills put up a shot just beyond Jeffrey's outstretched hand and the ball went through the net to tie the score. It was Mills' sixteenth point; the most he had ever scored in a game.

He heard Jeffrey say, "Lucky shot, you little queer."

Mills had to remind himself once again to bite his tongue. He kept his thoughts to himself: Go to hell, hawk face.

The score was tied, with thirty seconds left on the clock. The winner would advance to the high school state tournament.

Jeffrey dribbled the ball out front, letting the clock run down so he could take the last shot. When the clock ticked down to twenty seconds, Mills inched up to him. He watched the ball bouncing high and slow under Jeffrey's hand. Jeffrey was watching the clock and paid almost no attention to Mills.

At seventeen seconds, Mills had inched up so close he felt he could poke the ball away. When Jeffrey glanced at the clock again, Mills stabbed at the ball, tapping it cleanly. Jeffrey looked down at Mills, stunned. The ball bounced away into the empty end of the court. They both darted after it.

Mills was faster and scooped up the ball. With Jeffrey on his hip, he dribbled once, then went up and laid it in for the go-ahead basket. Mills fell to the floor. There was a terrific roar from the crowd, like the bleachers were collapsing. He was going to win the game. He was going to win the game.

There were eight seconds left. Woodlawn inbounded the ball to Jeffrey and he rushed it upcourt. Coach yelled at Mills to "Get back, get back."

Mills sprinted and caught up with Jeffrey at midcourt. Four seconds. Mills was in front of Jeffrey when Jeffrey made a stutter step to the right, setting Mills off balance. He reversed his dribble and got around Mills, jumping up high on his shot.

Mills reached for the ball, but instead slapped Jeffrey's free arm. Jeffrey fell to the floor from the contact. He rolled over to see what would happen. The ball bounced off the backboard, rimmed around the goal and fell through the basket.

The roar grew even louder. It was an angry reply from the Woodlawn fans. No one heard the buzzer or the referee's whistle. The referee pointed at Mills. Jeffrey would be awarded a free throw with no time on the clock for a chance to win the game. Once the crowd figured out what was happening, there were boos at one end and whistles and screams at the other.

Jeffrey stepped up to the line and nervously let the ball fly toward the goal. Swish. Woodlawn fans and the bench spilled onto the court, surrounding Jeffrey and the rest of the team in celebration.

Mills and his teammates stood separately and awkwardly, trying to digest what just happened. Mills knelt on one knee. He was exhausted. He tried to cry but couldn't. He tried to be mad but he wasn't. He wasn't even upset. He had played so well; the best he had ever played.

He stood up and watched Jeffrey as he was hoisted above the crowd and seated on a pair of shoulders. His red, sweaty face was smiling and laughing. Mills did not like that hawk face, but his earlier feeling of hatred had subsided. He wasn't even angry. It was more shock at the way it had ended after he thought he had won the game.

Mills knew he had played well against Jeffrey – again. The first time had been the previous year in a high school golf match. They had been paired together, and he and Jeffrey had almost fought because they couldn't stand each other.

In that match, Mills had shot his lowest-ever round for nine holes. Now he had played his best-ever basketball game, and again it was against Jeffrey. He didn't understand the connection, but he was certain there was one. Jeffrey brought out the best in him. That was evident. He didn't hate him. No. He knew he didn't hate him.

Mills started toward the celebration. He wanted to reach Jeffrey. He wasn't sure what he would do when he reached him; offer his hand most likely and congratulate him. He waded through the celebrants, his red-and-blue jersey standing out among the mass of black-and-gold.

The crowd was thickest toward the middle, like a knot. Jeffrey was let down on the court and the team and the crowd headed for the corner of the gym. The crowd trailed along behind them like the tail of a comet. It was impossible for Mills to reach Jeffrey, so he turned around and walked to his own locker room.

His teammates untucked their jerseys from their shorts and used them to wipe their eyes and faces. Their heads were bowed. Mills tried to act hurt and upset along with them, but it was no use. Inside, he was jumpy and reeling. He wasn't upset. He wasn't upset at all.

MILLWORM AND THE HAWK

During second hour at school, Charlie Mills heard a rumor that he would be number-one golfer for the match that afternoon. He was always number three on the team.

He imagined stepping to the first tee as the top golfer. He pictured the two teams standing beside each other on the tee box, the coaches standing before them getting ready to make the announcement. His insides turned hollow thinking about the first shot, which would have to be struck in front of everyone.

School dragged on and on that day, with endless lecturing and then an empty study hall with no homework to do. The hands on the clock would not budge. He had had time to consider the rumor critically, and it didn't make sense. He had turned in the best scores recently, but he wasn't the best golfer on the team. Triple Meat was.

Triple Meat's real name was Patrick Dunne. He had been hefty since he was little and everyone called him by his nickname, "Triple Meat and Cheese."

Mills wasn't even the second-best golfer. B.C. was. B.C. stood for Barry Collins and he was a smaller version of Triple Meat. Triple Meat and B.C. had struggled on the course recently. They had begun goofing off before the matches and their play had suffered for it. Perhaps Coach Hager was trying to send a message by promoting Mills.

After the last bell, Mills rushed to the golf course so he could practice putting before the match. He was a serious golfer now. On the drive over he noticed how strange the weather was acting. When the sun was out, the hills and small farms seemed to awaken in response to its warmth. Then a heavy, slow-moving cloud would roll in front of the sun, making it dark out like at dusk. A cold gust almost blew his little hatchback off the road, but when the sun peeked through again, the wind died.

Close to the road were small, rectangular-cut fields waiting for tobacco setting. The fields were black from being freshly plowed. He admired how the rectangles curved with the hill. Far off, sitting on top of a hill, stood a black barn he hadn't noticed before. Another heavy cloud moved in front of the sun and the fields grew dark again, followed by another burst of wind. Mills watched the trees bend in the gusts. When the wind died, the trees stood up straight again. He felt professionally prepared for the match, having observed the elements.

At the golf course the parking lot was mostly empty. He parked on the front row next to Triple Meat's rusted-out truck. He didn't see B.C.'s Camaro and figured they had ridden together. Since they weren't on the practice green or range, this meant they were in the locker room going through the members' golf bags, searching for a bottle for a snort.

Mills pulled his golf bag out of the hatchback and set it down carefully on the pavement. He flipped off his shoes and changed into golf spikes. He spoke to himself: "The number-one golfer has just arrived at Lone Oak Country Club. He's putting on his spikes."

There was no one on the practice putting green. Mills dropped two golf balls into the rough and chipped on. He was putting when he heard the squeak of the door to the pro shop opening. Triple Meat and B.C. came out, laughing about something. Mills watched them out of the corner of his eye. With their similar builds and Triple Meat towering over B.C., they looked like father and son. Mills turned his back to them but listened as they approached the green.

"Millllll-worrrrrm," Triple Meat said playfully.

"Hey, girls," Mills said without looking up. He felt embarrassed by the rumor. It was silly to think he would be number one.

Triple Meat and B.C. dropped some balls onto the putting green. Triple Meat yelled out, "Serbia!" They had learned in history that day of Serbia's involvement in starting the First World War. Triple Meat screamed again, "Serbia!" and putted wildly using one hand. He laughed until he choked.

Mills continued to practice seriously.

"Did you hear coach changed the seeding?" Triple Meat asked Mills.

"No. What is it?"

"You're number one."

"Are you serious?" Mills stopped and looked up at him.

"Yeah. I'm two and B.C. is three. Coach told me in study hall."

"That's stupid," Mills said.

"Why? You've had the lowest score the last two matches."

"So? A forty-one and a forty-three. You can beat that easily."

"I didn't."

"Well, you're still the best. You should be number one."

"Oh, it don't matter, Millworm."

Triple Meat made another comment to B.C. about Serbia and poked him in the neck with the end of the putter handle. Triple Meat took off running toward the pro shop. It was a spectacular sight to see his big body bouncing sloppily over the green. B.C. took off after him, screaming.

Mills had the putting green to himself again. *I'm the number-one golfer on the team*, he said to himself with great reverence. The honor was of no real consequence. In high school golf, a team consists of six or seven players, but only the top five scores of a nine-hole match are counted. So the number-one golfer could theoretically have his score scratched. But still, it was nice to be considered the top player on your team and to be matched with the opposing team's best player.

The Woodlawn golf team drove up in two black-and-gold vans with "Yellow Jackets" painted on both sides. The team emptied out of the vans wearing matching black-and-gold uniforms. The coach wore a black-and-gold jumpsuit. Mills stood watching as the Woodlawn players pulled golf bags out of the back of the vans. Each bag had a player's name stitched along the side.

Woodlawn had won several regional titles recently. *Big deal*, Mills thought. *I guess they think they're something.*

The Woodlawn players set their golf bags down on the apron of the practice green. There were about ten of them on the team. Half the team pulled out irons and headed for the driving range, while the other half practiced putting. The team looked serious and attended to the business of the day. Mills was a little intimidated since he was the only member of the host team outside practicing. Woodlawn had taken over without any resistance.

Mills noticed that all of the Woodlawn golfers had cocky-looking, rich-boy faces. The tallest member had blond hair cut short at the front and left long and stringy at the back. His eyes were sunk back in his head and he had a long, sharp, hooked nose. The short hair at the front, along with the sunken eyes and the hooked nose, made him look like a hawk.

The hawk stepped onto the putting green and caught Mills staring at him. Mills looked away, but it was too late. When he checked to see if he had been caught, he saw that the hawk was staring back at him predatorily. The hawk looked as if he might say something stupid like "What are you looking at?" but he didn't say anything. He dropped three golf balls and began putting. *I bet he's a punk*, Mills thought.

The coaches called the teams to the first tee to begin the match. Mills stood alongside Triple Meat, B.C. and the three sophomores who had shown up just in time to tee off. Down from them was the Woodlawn team, standing together holding their bags in front of them. They had twelve members lined up. The hawk stood over a bag with the name "Jeffrey Merritt" written on it.

Woodlawn's coach broke away from his team and walked onto the tee box. Facing everyone, he made this announcement: "Teeing first for Woodlawn today will be Jeffrey Merritt."

The Woodlawn players applauded as Jeffrey pulled out a driver and walked to the tee carrying a shiny new golf ball and a black tee. The applause died when he pushed the tee into the ground. The home team turned to look at each other and made faces.

Jeffrey stood over the ball a long time, just looking at it. Still blowing in gusts, the wind settled for him nicely. He drew the club back slowly and, with a swift follow-through, ripped the ball cleanly and solidly. The ball soared high and grew smaller and smaller in the sky. The ball had a slight draw that, after landing, rolled to the left center of the fairway. Everyone stood watching the drive. Mills was impressed with how coolly Jeffrey had handled the pressure of hitting first. Jeffrey quickly picked up the unbroken tee, shoved it into his pocket and walked over to stand beside his teammates.

Mills waited for Coach Hager's introduction. Coach Hager looked his team over and said, "Charlie, get over there and hit. You're going first today."

Mills, walking hurriedly to the tee, glanced back at his teammates to whisper, "What, no applause?"

Triple Meat grinned and pressed his middle finger against his leg.

That's about right for us, Mills thought.

He took a couple of practice swings, and after doing so realized Jeffrey hadn't taken any and felt a little inferior for it. The wind picked up and was blowing in his face. He smelled rain in the air. He thought about all the eyes that were watching him. He thought of Coach Hager and how he was probably just praying for a respectable drive.

He addressed the ball and waggled the head of the club, trying to get a good feel for the club and its potential. When he brought the club back for the real thing he became concerned with the mechanics of his swing. *Is the club parallel to the ground? How do my legs look? Am I delivering proper weight distribution? Are my feet lined up for the fairway?* He wondered if his arms looked like a pretzel.

His eyes were down on the ball, but his inner eye was scanning all over his body, hoping everything looked good. He followed through and heard a hollow wump. That's the sound it makes when the ball has been topped. He had struck the ball with the manufacturer's plate on the bottom of the club. The ball jumped up and then shot back down, settling into rough just past the end of the tee box.

Someone giggled and then choked it off.

He bent down to gather his broken tee, then went over to his bag. Leaning down, he threw the driver hard into it.

"Dammit," Mills grunted, punching his leg.

Triple Meat came over to Mills. "Oh, don't worry about it," he said, patting Mills' back sincerely.

Mills picked up his bag forcefully and slung it over his shoulder, making a racket. Jeffrey had already started walking ahead. Without turning around or stopping, he pointed down at the rough to show Mills his ball.

Thanks a lot, you shit, Mills thought. *I can see it from here. It was never out of sight.*

Mills pulled out a three-wood, slung the bag down and looked back at the tee box to see how far the ball had traveled. His teammates were smiling; he was close enough to see their teeth. Everyone continued to watch him from the tee box. He wanted to beat the hell out of the ball.

When he looked up the fairway, Jeffrey had moved to the far left side and was walking backwards, keeping an eye on him. The ball was buried pretty deep in the rough. It would be difficult to pop the ball out with a three-wood, so he switched to a five-iron and, connecting heavily, punched the ball into the fairway. Mills felt better. He had made a good decision. The first hole was a short par four. All Mills had to do now was knock it onto the green and one-putt or two-putt for a par or a bogey. The first hole wasn't going to be a disaster after all.

Both hit their approaches onto the green, leaving Jeffrey with a putt for birdie and Mills with a putt for par. Mills noticed how smoothly Jeffrey's putt rolled on the green. The ball appeared to be dead center of the cup, but it cut away at the end and lipped out.

"Nice putt, Jeffrey," Mills said. It was the first time either had spoken. "Do you prefer Jeff or Jeffrey?"

Jeffrey did not acknowledge the compliment or answer the question.

Mills had an eight-footer downhill, and since Jeffrey's putt broke at the end he allowed for it. When the ball slid into the cup he felt like jumping up and down and circling the green, waving the putter in the air. And since Jeffrey hadn't responded to him, Mills felt like pointing the putter in his face, screaming, "Yeah, that par was all in your face!" But Mills didn't actually do any of these things. He only thought about them while Jeffrey tapped in for par.

"Nice par," Mills said, writing a four on Jeffrey's scorecard.

Jeffrey pulled Mills' scorecard out of his back pocket and said, "What did you have?"

You son of a bitch, Mills thought. *You don't know?* Then he said aloud, "You don't know?"

"No. What did you have?"

What an asshole, Mills thought, shaking his head. He didn't answer. He simply lifted his clubs over his shoulder and walked past Jeffrey.

Jeffrey followed Mills toward the second tee. "Do you want your score kept or not? I'll just throw your scorecard in the trash can if you want."

Mills stopped and turned around. "I had a par, you prick. Just like you."

Jeffrey stopped and looked at him. Out came the hawk face. The hawk had a menacing stare. The hawk looked as if he wanted to either curse or throw a punch. Instead, he brought the scorecard up and wrote on it. Then he took off toward the row of bushy pine trees that hid the second tee.

A nervous, shaky feeling coursed through Mills. It always did after a confrontation. He watched Jeffrey disappear behind the last pine. Jeffrey had a muscular thickness about him and was a little taller and broader than Mills. But Mills felt pretty good about his own toughness. He wondered how things would turn out in a fight. He wondered if Jeffrey would throw a punch if provoked enough. He probably had some scrap to him.

On the second tee, Jeffrey swung the driver slowly and beautifully and maintained his balance after the follow-through. The ball went high and straight, cutting the center of the fairway.

"Nice drive." It was a habit for Mills to compliment a good shot. The compliment sounded strange after he had just called Jeffrey a prick.

Jeffrey's face reddened. He picked up his bag and slammed the driver into it. "Listen, can we not comment, please?"

Mills was on the tee now and looked back at Jeffrey.

"Can't you just play and not talk?" Jeffrey asked.

"What an asshole," Mills said, turning around to look down the fairway. He could tell Jeffrey was about to respond, so he waited before swinging. He half expected a jab to the back of the head.

"Just top the ball so we can keep moving."

Inside, Mills was burning. Jeffrey had scorched him with a pretty good one. Mills stepped away from the ball. "You're a hook-nosed, country club faggot, you know that?" He knew his comeback wasn't as good.

"You're calling me names? Are you in the third grade?"

Mills went back to the ball and swung the club about as hard as he could, losing his balance in the process. Hit solidly, the ball landed hot in the fairway and rolled past Jeffrey's drive.

"Lick on that!" Mills shouted to Jeffrey, who had already started walking. Jeffrey ignored the comment. *What a dumb thing to say*, Mills thought. *If that's the best I can do I should just keep my mouth shut.*

On the walk to their drives, Mills studied Jeffrey's long, graceful stride. Each stride was long enough for a dog to run between his legs. *He probably thinks he's a pro. He probably thinks I'm his caddie.*

All through the round, Mills and Jeffrey consistently hit good shots down the middle and chipped onto the green. Every time Jeffrey hit a good shot, Mills would think about his next shot and study his club selection more than ever before. He played smart and didn't let his mind wander.

His putting had always been his biggest problem because he tended to rush it. But against Jeffrey he slowed everything down, read the line and tried to make the ball roll as smoothly across the green as Jeffrey's did. Mills stopped talking altogether after the exchange on the second tee. No more compliments, no more comments. Nothing.

They both parred the first five holes, something Mills had never done before. He couldn't believe how well he was playing.

The sixth was a long, tough par four. If he could just par it, Mills would have a good chance at shooting in the thirties. And if he birdied one of the remaining holes he could maybe shoot one-under. That would be unthinkable. He had only broken forty once in his life, and that was because he had made a fifty-foot birdie putt on the ninth for a thirty-nine.

On the sixth green, Mills missed a short par putt and Jeffrey made his to take a one-stroke lead. Mills scolded himself for dreaming about some make-believe score. He had let his mind wander. He went back to thinking only of the next shot and trying to match Jeffrey shot for shot.

Mills remained a stroke back going into the ninth, the final hole of the match. He missed the green, chipped up close to the pin and putted out for par. He felt elated that his wonderful round was over. There was nothing more to do and no way to wreck it. His giddiness was hard to contain. He stood just off the green out of Jeffrey's way so Jeffrey could concentrate on a difficult twenty-five foot downhill putt for birdie.

As soon as Jeffrey putted, Mills knew he had hit it too hard. Jeffrey's only hope was for the ball to hit some part of the cup to slow it down and keep it from going all the way to the bottom of the green. The ball rolled three inches right of the cup and picked up speed downhill. The ball came to rest on the fringe, thirty feet away. Inside, Mills was jumping up and down, going crazy. If Jeffrey two-putted from there they were tied. If he three-putted, which was a strong possibility, Mills would win the match.

Jeffrey showed no signs of a choke. He set the flagstick back into the cup and walked over to his ball with long, slow-moving strides, as if he had planned to miss the putt that badly. He lined up the putt, took a couple of practice strokes, then, with a long, smooth stroke, putted the ball firmly and confidently. The ball rolled as if it were in a groove to the cup. The ball rattled the flagstick, momentarily lodging between the flagstick and the lip of the cup, then dropped in.

Jeffrey raised the putter over his head and smiled back at an imaginary gallery.

Mills had watched the putt all the way. When the ball dropped he felt as though the air had been knocked out of him, like the times when he had landed flat on his back in football. He punched his leg. *What a lucky bastard he is.*

After each match it is customary for competitors to shake hands. Since he felt Jeffrey was a jerk, an SOB and a lucky bastard, Mills did not congratulate him or offer his hand. Instead, he gathered his bag and took off for the clubhouse.

Jeffrey quickly pulled his bag over his shoulder and took off at a jog, his clubs clanging with each step. Jeffrey rushed over to his coach, who was on the driving range working with the players who had not played in the match. Mills heard him tell his coach that he had shot even par, and he sounded very excited by it. *Yeah*, Mills thought, *don't forget to tell him what an asshole you are.*

Mills finished one-over for a thirty-seven. He said it aloud: "Thirty-seven." The feeling of accomplishment trumped the bitterness he had felt throughout the match, though he knew he would never be able to think of the round without remembering how he had lost to that hawk face, Jeffrey.

The cart path he was on led to the storage building. Standing in the opening of the wide garage was Coach Hager. Mills walked up to him and told him his score. Coach Hager did not look impressed.

"Is that right?" Coach Hager spat on the grass. He looked as though he hadn't heard what Mills had said, or as though there was something else on his mind.

Mills propped his golf bag on a rack. "That's the best I've ever played in my life."

"What did the Woodlawn boy shoot?"

"Oh, he was even. He was such a lucky ..." Mills didn't finish his sentence.

"Hmm. Beat you by one stroke. Well, that's tough. Did you congratulate him?"

"Yeah."

"You did? You shook his hand and congratulated him on a fine match?"

"Sure."

"No you didn't. I watched you two finish from up there." He pointed to the dining room over the pro shop. Mills looked up to see the sliding glass door that overlooked the patio, the swimming pool and the ninth green.

"Well, he was a jerk."

"He was? What did he do?"

"I don't know. He was just snotty-acting."

"Charlie, you congratulate your opponent after a match. Period."

Mills wanted to defend his actions, but he couldn't think of what to say.

"You conduct yourself like a gentleman out there. Don't be a sore loser. I don't want a spoilsport."

Mills hated the word "spoilsport." He had heard it said many times.

Coach Hager saw how hurt Mills was by the reprimand. "Ah, hell, Charlie, at least somebody finally played well. What happened? Were you concentrating?"

"Yeah," Mills said. "I wanted to beat him so bad."

"Charlie," Coach Hager shook his head in disgust. "Don't be like that. Don't ... Just play the golf course. Don't pay any attention to your opponent."

Mills spotted Jeffrey and the Woodlawn coach on the cart path walking toward them. Coach Hager also saw them coming. Something was up.

"What's this, Charlie? I swear, if you've embarrassed the school somehow ..."

"He was the jerk. I didn't do nothing."

Jeffrey and the Woodlawn coach came up and stopped in front of Mills. The Woodlawn coach smiled suddenly and asked, "You got Jeffrey's scorecard?"

"Yes, sir," Mills said, handing it to him.

"You got mine?" Mills asked Jeffrey.

"Oh, right," Jeffrey said, pulling the card out of his back pocket.

"What did you have on nine?" Jeffrey asked.

"A hole in one."

Jeffrey pulled a face at his coach. "See. He's been like this the whole time."

"Charlie!" Coach Hager shouted.

"I had a par."

Jeffrey wrote in a four, added up the score and handed Mills the card.

"What did you shoot, son?" the Woodlawn coach asked Mills.

"One-over."

"Well done," he said, offering his hand. Mills shook it. Mills could see that Jeffrey didn't like his coach congratulating him.

"Looks like we got us a couple of fine golfers," the Woodlawn coach smiled at Coach Hager.

"That's a heckuva match they played there," Coach Hager said. He stepped toward Jeffrey and patted him on the back awkwardly, then fumbled for his hand and shook it.

The coaches looked at both boys. Mills could tell Coach Hager was waiting for him to congratulate Jeffrey on the match, but he didn't budge. He glanced up at Jeffrey, who looked as if he might break into a pout if he were made to stand there any longer.

Mills wanted to smack Jeffrey's stupid, sulking, smart-ass, snotty, lucky, rich-boy face. He wanted to slap his face hard with an open hand. Slapping that sissy face seemed more appropriate than punching it.

"Jeffrey," the Woodlawn coach said and nodded toward Mills.

Jeffrey repositioned the clubs on his shoulder and then took off walking toward the parking lot. The three of them stood there watching as he walked away.

The Woodlawn coach cleared his throat and said, "I'd like to apologize for Jeffrey's behavior." He looked at Mills and then at Coach Hager. "Jeffrey's a good golfer but he's not a very good sport. I'm working with him on that. I've told him he doesn't have to like his opponent, but he must be polite and use good manners. He should appreciate the fact that his opponent brings out his competitive nature. That's when he plays his best golf. He must have really been sore at you, son, because that's his best score this year."

"Mine, too," Mills said and smiled.

"Jeffrey's not the only one to blame," Coach Hager said. "My boy's just as much at fault."

"That may be so, but I asked Jeffrey to come over here and shake hands. It's easier to be a good sport when you've won. Being a good loser, now that's tough. I can't even get Jeffrey to be a good winner. He's got a lot of anger. But it's that anger, I think, that helps him to perform. If you're one of those who plays well when you're mad you should, in essence, thank your opponent for bringing out that performance. When you shake hands at the end you're really thanking him for spurring you on to great play. But I can't get Jeffrey to see it that way. I tell him all the time: hate inwardly but be polite outwardly."

The Woodlawn coach winked at both of them and then walked back to the driving range to work with his players.

"See, I told you Jeffrey was a jerk," Mills said to Coach Hager.

"He was describing you, too, Charlie."

"What? I'm not like that."

"If you can't shake that boy's hand, you're a sore loser."

"I'm not a sore loser."

"Sure you are. And I'll kick you off this team if you can't act right. I expect you to shake hands with your opponent every match. No exceptions!"

Mills wasn't comfortable arguing with an adult, so he bit his tongue. They walked together to the ninth green and watched the rest of the matches come in. He was hoping Triple Meat and B.C. would come in with victories so they would beat Woodlawn. While they waited, he thought of the short putt he had missed on six and all the birdie opportunities he had blown.

Triple Meat and B.C. came in with two of the worst scores they had ever carded. They had both shot in the high forties. Coach Hager shook his head and chuckled as he read the scorecards. Woodlawn took all five matches and won in a rout.

In the pro shop, Mills found Triple Meat and B.C. at the counter buying candy bars. Mills went up to them. "What happened out there?" he asked.

"You should have seen B.C. on seven," Triple Meat said. "I was getting ready to tee off on eight when I heard a ball go 'bloop' into the water. I looked up and there was B.C. dropping a ball down. Then 'bloop', he did it again."

"So? You hit it in the water on eight," B.C. replied.

"I know, I know. I was right there with you, buddy," he laughed.

"God, I'd be sick if I played like that," Mills said.

Triple Meat looked at B.C. "Listen at Nicklaus over here."

"No, I didn't mean it like that. I meant I would've hated playing that bad in front of those punks. Weren't they the biggest jerkwads?"

"I don't know," Triple Meat said. "I didn't notice."

"You didn't think they were the snottiest little faggots you'd ever seen in your life?"

"What are you talking about?"

"That punk I played with. I wanted to kick his ass."

"Oh, you're just mad 'cause you got beat."

"No I'm not. He was an asshole."

"Yes you are. You're a sore loser."

"No I'm not. He was a prick."

"You're just a sore loser. Ain't he, B.C.?"

B.C. shrugged his shoulders.

"I'm not a sore loser," Mills said.

"Yes you are."

"No I'm not."

"You have a heart attack about everything. You make a big damn deal out of everything. Don't he, B.C.?"

B.C. shrugged his shoulders again.

"No I don't," Mills said.

"Yes you do."

Mills shook his head and walked out. He put his clubs into the trunk and sat in the car. *Listen to them in there*, he thought. *They don't even care. What do they care about? Nothing. Look at their scores. They're terrible. Then they come in laughing about it. What a bunch of turds. What a bunch of chok-ing turds.* It was no use. What good was it to bad-mouth Triple Meat and B.C.? Mills did not like thinking badly of his friends. He liked them and didn't want to be angry with them.

He thought the day had been ruined because of Jeffrey. *Jeffrey was to blame. Jeffrey ruined it by being a jerk and a lucky bastard. No,* he thought. *He did not ruin the day. It was a good day and just because he was a jerk didn't mean you had to be a jerk. Why did you have to make an ass of yourself?*

Mills knew he had behaved badly. He had always responded that way to punks and had always been a sore loser. It was embarrassing to think back to all the times he had lost at something, lost his cool and acted rot-ten. He always felt it was wrong to act like that. He hated that he was a sore loser.

Mills vowed to apologize to Coach Hager and to promise to congrat-ulate his opponent after every match. He thought about what the Wood-lawn coach had said about hating your opponent inwardly while being polite outwardly. *I wonder if I can feel one way and act another. Sounds easier said than done.*

Chapter VIII

On January 1, 2000, two worthless golfers and I played a round at the Griffin Gate Marriott Resort. On the first hole I tapped in for birdie. Now, I'm a fair golfer who has had his share of birdies, but a birdie coming at the start of a round, the first day of a new century, carried some significance. No? Perhaps this was the dawn of great things to come for me in golf. Alas, two holes later I double-bogeyed and the round spiraled out of control.

My two companions played dreadfully. They pounded the earth repeatedly, producing only a trickle from the golf ball.

It was a mild day; really fine weather for golf. Sixty degrees. The sun hid behind clouds and would peep out occasionally to give the course color. Since the round was going badly for all of us, I tried to concentrate on enjoying being outdoors on a warm winter's day.

Then the rain and the wind came. Before long my grips were wet and my hands were cold. My only towel was soaked. By the time we reached the back nine I was ready to quit. On the fourteenth hole someone suggested getting a drink afterward. Aha. Things were looking up again. Nothing brings joy like the prospect of a drink after work, or exercise, or just the end of a day.

We finished all eighteen holes, put our clubs in the car and walked across the parking lot and tennis courts to the resort hotel. Inside, you could smell the chlorine from the swimming pool and hear the fountain splashing. After some searching, we found a small bar that was more like a disco lounge with its heavy-cushioned seats and small, round tables. We sat at the bar and ordered Canadian beer, which we poured into glasses. It felt like a vacation.

"Ahh, that tastes good," one said.

"Has it ever not tasted good?" the other replied.

"The American beer we had last night at that Chinese place wasn't very good."

The beer went down very smoothly indeed. We watched a football game on a set behind the bar. We didn't talk much. After two beers I looked over at the worthless golfers. They both appeared to be thinking and looked a little gloomy.

"I suppose I should be going soon," one said.

"Yeah, my family won't start dinner until I get home."

I, too, had a family, but I wasn't thinking about them at this moment. "Tell me about when you guys used to work at 803 South," I said to them.

"Oh, you've heard all of that before," one said.

"Well, what about when you were locked up in the john all night? Talk about that."

"Nah, you've heard it plenty of times. C'mon, let's go."

The football game was in the third quarter. I mentioned that we should at least stay until the end of the game. They both stood up. I couldn't think of anything to say to get them to stay longer, so I also stood up.

We paid our bill and left. Frost was right when he wrote 'Nothing Gold Can Stay.'

THE FIRST CUT

The McConnell boys – Adam, Peter, Paul, Michael, Joseph and Johnny – all played basketball in the winter. They played baseball, golf and tennis in the spring and summer, and football in the fall. They played in different leagues at different levels, and their parents tried to watch a little of all the games.

Afterward, the boys would come home and toss their dirty uniforms down the basement steps. Sleeves and pant legs dangled off the side of the staircase for days until their mother picked them up on wash day.

Then the boys would gather in the living room and wait for Adam to move the ottoman into the kitchen to clear floor space. He would be first to re-enact his triumphs and would often include one or more of his brothers in the replay. Each one got a chance to replay his exploits. Those who hadn't had a good performance remained quiet, but it was rare that a brother had nothing to share.

The boys left a trail of wreckage all over the house: abandoned shoes, socks, toys, pillows, blankets and assorted balls. Their mother would clean it all up at night and have everything put back in its place, only for the boys to create another mess the next day.

Their mother always had a big dinner prepared every night, and the boys would eat with ravenous hunger. Meat and potatoes were their favorite. It could be any kind of beef or chicken and any kind of potato. Baked or mashed, it didn't matter. But if their mother tried to introduce a green vegetable, it was sneered at and shunned.

After dinner, while their mother attended to the dishes, the boys would go out into the backyard and resume a suspended game or start a new one.

A fight would inevitably break out and by then it was late enough for all of the boys to be sent to bed.

Their only real responsibility was school and church, and they attended both begrudgingly. As soon as they were excused from either, it was playtime.

Whenever the boys were home, be it after school or church or during summer break, they could never sit still. There were always games to be played. Johnny, the baby brother, never had to think of what to do. Boredom simply didn't exist. He would just see what his brothers were up to and join their escapades.

Games would start inside the house. They would play slow-motion football in the living room, but then someone would get tackled so hard by accident that his head would bounce on the floor, and in that house any kind of fall sounded like someone had dropped a sixteen-pound bowling ball. The hit would shake the foundations. Their parents would rush in and ask who did what. No one would ever accuse or confess, so all the boys would be ordered outside.

They would sit in the bare spot under the red maple tree in the back-yard and punch each other until someone finally suggested Wiffle ball or football. Adam always took the two youngest, Joe and Johnny, and they would play against Peter, Paul and Michael. They played until the ball struck a window. If the window broke, they were all in trouble. If the window didn't break, the sound of a plastic Wiffle ball or a football hitting glass was loud enough to stir their parents out of their chairs to rap on an upstairs window and signal for them to either come back inside or get lost.

II

Adam was the first to go away to college. This struck a blow to the house-hold. It was never the same after Adam left. Johnny could sense the angst in the family; the brothers weren't as consumed with playing games any more. His mother and father seemed sullen. It was only natural for the boys to grow up and move on, but no one had ever discussed this eventuality.

Not long after that, Peter moved out. Paul followed next and then it was Michael's turn. Johnny was fifteen when the last of the brothers,

Joseph, moved out. Johnny would come home from school and it was always sad to find the house empty and quiet enough to hear the house creak.

He tried not to think about his brothers being gone because he was a sophomore in high school and it was October, and he was about to go out for the basketball team. All of his brothers had played high school ball. Johnny wanted to make the team more than anything else, and he felt good about his chances. Watching his brothers play high school ball had been the best, and he liked to imagine what it would be like playing on the team. He used to picture himself wearing the red uniform like his brothers, but it all seemed too far away to ever come true.

He had played the guard position for the school's basketball teams in the seventh, eighth and ninth grades. He had started some games, but he mostly came off the bench as the sixth man. All three of his junior high school coaches referred to him as the team's spark plug: "Whenever we need a lift, we put Johnny into the game. Something always happens when he's in there: a steal, a basket, something," the coaches would say in the locker room in front of the whole team. This led Johnny to wonder why he wasn't a starter, but it didn't bother him too much because he played as many minutes as the starters, and in some cases more.

After the first week of tryouts, Johnny wasn't worried. He had made it past the first two rounds of cuts. When the list of players making the second cut was posted on the bulletin board in the library, Johnny wrote down every name. He took the list home and read over the names carefully at the desk in his room. There he trimmed the list down to twelve varsity players and twelve junior varsity players. He thought that the teams he came up with were the best teams possible, and he had included himself on the junior varsity team.

The final round of cuts came at the conclusion of practice on a Friday. Varsity Coach Gregor Bottoms gathered everyone out of bounds by the rollaway bleachers that were stacked next to the locker room. First, he called the names of the players who made varsity. Whenever a player's name was called, the player jumped up and jogged into the locker room. The only sound made was their soles squeaking on the court.

Then Coach Bottoms called out the names of the players who had made junior varsity. All of the good players who were Johnny's teammates in junior high got called. Each shouted out a whoop and ran into the locker room; some slapping the side of the bleachers. Johnny grew anxious after each name was called.

Coach Bottoms looked up from the clipboard. "OK, boys, that's it. Thanks for coming out."

Johnny hadn't heard his name called. It had all happened so fast. Perhaps he had missed his name when it was called. He got up and walked toward the locker room, keeping Coach Bottoms in his peripheral vision to see if he would come up to him. Coach Bottoms didn't.

Johnny pushed open the door to the locker room and circled the middle of the floor near the drain. He contemplated confronting the coach to see if there was a mistake. Tommy Arnold, a senior, was standing at his locker stripped down to his jock strap, twisting a towel into a tight roll. Tommy flicked the towel, which was wet at one end, at Johnny, striking his leg. A stinging sensation flared up quickly. Johnny looked at Tommy. Tommy was friends with his older brothers. He had known Tommy forever.

"What's wrong, Little Mac?" Tommy asked.

Johnny just looked at him. "I don't know."

Johnny circled the drain again. He couldn't decide what to do. He went over and sat down on the bench in front of his locker. There he changed out of his wet T-shirt, shorts and socks. Everything smelled old and sweaty. The whole locker room smelled like feet and sweat. He pulled on his blue jeans, dry socks, a dry T-shirt and tennis shoes, and threw on a sweatshirt. Steam was coming from the showers and he could hear the water smacking the tiles. The shower room echoed with shouts and cheers. The ones who had been cut did not bother to shower. Many of them didn't even change. They simply grabbed their bags and books and took off.

Johnny hurried to finish dressing before the players came out of the shower. He didn't want to see them. Two players, Jimmy and Kenny, who he had known would make the team and whom he liked very much, he did not want to see at all. He certainly didn't want to congratulate them and then hear them say: "Sorry you didn't make the team."

He heard people coming out of the shower and avoided looking their way. He fixed his gaze on the locker door he closed, the vent cuts in the door, the combination locks hanging from the other lockers, the two brown benches, the gray floor with the drain in the middle, the light switch on the wall, the brown locker room door and the brass handle he pulled toward him, the side of the stacked bleachers on his left and the empty basketball court.

There at the far end under the basket stood Coach Bottoms. He was talking to another boy who had been cut. The coach was looking down at the clipboard in his hand, and was showing it to the boy. The boy shook his head and started for the double doors next to the red wall padding. Johnny had to know. He had to hear it from Coach Bottoms. He stopped in front of the coach.

"Oh, hello, Johnny," Coach Bottoms said.

"Is my name on the list? My name is Johnny McConnell." His voice sounded as if it were coming out of his ears.

"I know you, Johnny buddy. I coached some of your brothers. I'm sorry, Johnny, but I just don't have a place for you. I've got a surplus of guards here." Bottoms showed him the clipboard and the list of JV players. Johnny read the names. He stopped at the names George Madison and Rob Koch.

"I can't believe it," Johnny said, reading over the names again.

"I'm sorry, Johnny."

"OK." He couldn't think of anything more to say.

He walked through the double doors, crossed the lobby, passing alongside the glass trophy case, and opened the doors at the front of the school. He sat on the low brick wall and leaned back against a pole. He had never been cut from any sport. He couldn't believe it. Basketball, too. He really couldn't believe it. He was better at basketball than all of the other sports. Basketball was his favorite.

He wiped his eyes and looked around to see if anyone had seen him crying. There were boys getting into cars in the pick-up line, but no one was waiting on the brick wall next to him, to his relief.

He thought of the list Coach Bottoms had showed him. Two names stuck out: George Madison and Rob Koch. Both were his age and both were guards. George Madison had always played behind Johnny in junior high. George was a good player and a good friend, but Johnny knew he was better than George. He was sure George knew it too.

Rob Koch was a surprise. Rob had moved from Ohio before school started and had told Johnny that he had never played organized basketball.

His sport was tennis. After watching him play, Johnny figured he would be cut in the first round. Then, when he wasn't, Johnny figured he'd be cut in the second round.

Johnny hadn't worried about Rob making the team because, for starters, he didn't know how to dribble. He kept his head down and slapped at the ball with both hands to keep it in front of him. On defense, his footing was all wrong. He couldn't defend without getting his hands all over you, fouling. He didn't jump well, either, and he looked awkward running up and down the court. His head made quick, jerky movements as he looked all over the court, wondering what was going on.

Johnny remembered Coach Bottoms making a big show of Rob's "perfect form" while shooting free throws midway through tryouts. He had stopped the practice and made everyone watch. Rob did have good form and he had swished the two free throws while everyone watched.

Is it possible, Johnny wondered, *that Rob Koch made the team because he was a good free throw shooter? The rest of his game was a mess. He would never get to the free throw line because no one would ever foul him, because no coach would ever put him in the game.*

He spotted his family's blue Oldsmobile pulling into the school. The car looked like a blue whale and had been with the family for ten years. It still had the sour smell in it from when a gallon of milk had leaked into the carpet years earlier, and no amount of washing and scrubbing would eliminate it. He could tell by the silhouette of hair that went as high as the roof that his mother was driving. Johnny opened the door and there it was: the smell of his mom's perfume along with the sour milk.

Johnny looked straight ahead. He ignored his mother's stare. Seeing Johnny's eyes puffy and red, she asked what was wrong. What had made him cry? She asked what had happened in tryouts. Had he made the team?

"You'd better talk to me, young man."

Johnny kept quiet.

"Please, honey, talk to your mother. Did you make the team?"

He shook his head.

"No?"

He shook his head again and looked down.

"You were cut?"

He nodded.

"Oh, my word. Well, it's OK, honey. Don't worry about it."

He stared straight ahead. Knowing that his father and brothers and everyone would eventually have to know made it even more devastating. This was really happening. He had seen the list. He had opened the double doors and Coach Bottoms had let him walk out.

His mother looked out at the road ahead as they approached an underpass, and by the way her eyes darted from side to side and the way she was being quiet it seemed she was upset by the news.

"What happened?" his mother asked.

"I don't know. I had a good tryout."

"Oh, honey. I'm so sorry. My goodness."

A minute passed and she started again: "What did Mr. Bottoms say to you?"

"Nothing really. He showed me the list and said he had too many guards and that he couldn't keep me."

"Did he say anything else?"

"No."

His mother smoothed his wet hair back and patted his shoulder. "It's OK, honey. Don't worry about it."

When they got home she told his father. His father knitted his eyebrows together and one corner of his mouth curled into a queer-looking frown. He looked at Johnny as if something sinister was afoot.

"What happened?" his father asked.

"I don't know. George Madison made the team and this new guy who plays tennis."

"George Madison? You're better than him."

"I know. Can't you do something?"

"What can be done?" his father asked. "The coach is going to keep who he wants. There's nothing I can do."

Johnny and his parents stood in the kitchen. They were thinking.

"George Madison," his father said contemptuously. "What's this other kid's name? The tennis player?"

"Rob Koch."

"Koch. Hmm. Koch."

"Do you know them?"

"No. Can't say I do."

"They just moved here from Ohio."

"Hmm. Is he any good?"

"No, he's awful. Worse than George."

"Hmm. All you can do is try again next year."

And that was that. Nothing more was said about it that night.

Every day for a week after the cut, Johnny peeked through the small windows of the gym doors to watch basketball practice. At the end of each practice, Coach Bottoms made the boys run lines. Afterward, the team walked under the basket and along the baseline with their hands on their hips and hung their heads between their shoulders, heaving and gasping for breath. Some kneeled on one knee. Johnny hated running line drills, but boy he'd love to run them now, harder and better than anyone else.

About a month later, his father came home from work and called Johnny and his mother into the kitchen. "I've got some news about your friend Rob Koch," his father said. "Turns out his father moved his family here from Ohio over the summer. He's a professor at the seminary. The school superintendent asked him to serve on the school board. So it looks to me like Gregor Bottoms is trying to protect his job by buttering up to a board member."

"Is his job in jeopardy?" his mother asked.

"As head basketball coach it is. He's had a losing record every year. He's had some pretty good teams, too."

"How is Rob Koch going to help him win?" Johnny asked.

"He's not, but he has assured himself of at least one vote in his favor should the board decide it's time to fire the coach. Johnny, you're a sacrificial lamb. He's willing to sacrifice you in order to save his own neck."

"Can't we do something about it? Let's go to the athletic director or the principal."

"Don't you think Bottoms will say that he genuinely feels Rob Koch is a better basketball player and that politics had nothing to do with it? We would have a hard time proving otherwise."

"There's got to be something we can do. It's not right," Johnny said. "It's just not right."

III

Johnny wondered what he would do after school now. Basketball was all he ever did in the winter. He was lost without it. If he was to make the team the following year, he would have to get better, and the only way to get better was to play, so he signed up for the city basketball league and was picked up by the Warriors.

There were only a few good players in the entire league. That year, he led the league in scoring, averaging more than twenty points a game. The Warriors won their division and league tournament. He had never been on a winning team before, and the games were played in front of a packed gym every night. The last time he had played in front of that many people had been in the eighth grade, when the school team had played a noon game in front of the student body.

League games were played on Wednesday nights, and once during the middle of the season, Johnny found himself excited about how well the team was doing. He dressed for the game, went downstairs and found his father sitting in the living room resting after dinner. He asked his dad if he was ready to drive him to the game.

"Do you mind walking?" his father asked. His eyes were closed and he was leaning back on the sofa with his feet up on the ottoman.

"You're not going to the game?"

"Nah, I don't think so."

"Why not? I like it when you're there."

"Well, it's just that it's a little demeaning. You know, sitting there in that elementary school gym watching you play in that league when I'm used to going to games at the high school. I don't know. I just don't care for it."

Johnny didn't say anything.

"I'll wait up for you tonight, OK? You can tell me how you did."

After the game, Johnny ran home from the gym and thought about the twenty-four points he had scored and how he would describe the scoring to his father. He made it home and looked in all the rooms downstairs, but no one was there, so he ran upstairs to his parents' bedroom.

"What is it, honey?" his mother said.

"Is Dad asleep?"

"Yes."

"I scored twenty-four points tonight."

"That's wonderful, honey."

"Don't tell Dad. I want to tell him in the morning."

"OK, honey."

The next morning, Johnny awoke and heard his father whistling downstairs in the kitchen. That meant he was making his breakfast. His mother no longer made breakfast now that all the boys were grown. She had started working in the office at an elementary school and was gone in the morning.

Johnny got up and ran downstairs. He found his father standing at the sink, dabbing his finger into the water under the faucet. He had burned it making coffee. Johnny told him he had scored twenty-four points the previous night and that they had beaten a very good team.

His father smiled politely. "Is that the most you've ever scored in a game?"

Johnny nodded. He was ready to describe each basket, when his father buttoned his overcoat and opened the door to the garage. "Off to work," he said. "Off to work."

The next Wednesday night, Johnny put on his uniform and sweats and went downstairs to ask his father to come to the game, but when he reached the living room his father was lying down and he could tell he was settled in for the night. He didn't want to become a nuisance, so he quit asking his father to the games and went ahead and walked to the gym.

IV

At the end of another losing high school basketball season, the school board went over the last five disappointing campaigns and voted to fire Coach Bottoms. He was kept on as a teacher because of his tenure. Every department had at least one ex-coach.

With the next basketball season came a new coach, Pete Strauss, who also was the high school tennis coach. Johnny was hopeful. He was now a junior and his goal was to make varsity, but if not, junior varsity would be fine. His main concern was making the team.

On the first day of tryouts, he noticed that Rob Koch wasn't there. The next day at school he asked Rob why. Rob told him he wasn't going out for basketball, that he was concentrating on tennis year-round.

Johnny breezed through the first two cuts, and on the final day of tryouts Coach Strauss paired up players and made them play one-on-one. Johnny was matched against George Madison. They clowned a bit at first, trying to make outrageous shots and moves. The game got serious at the end when the score was tied and the next basket would be the winner. Johnny had the ball and made a quick cut to the goal. He passed George on the dribble and went up for a layup. In an attempt to prevent him from scoring, George slapped Johnny hard across the wrists and flung him to the ground. The shot got off before he was hit and the ball banked in for the winning basket.

George helped Johnny to his feet and patted him on the back. "Good game, man," George said.

Later, Coach Strauss called off the names of the players who had made varsity. When Strauss called out Johnny's name, Johnny got up and walked into the locker room. He thought he would jump up and down and scream and throw a fist into the air. But suddenly he had no desire for any of it. He was happy, but he had no desire to make a show. He thought he would want to celebrate, but when the feeling didn't grab him he refused to do anything false or forced. He wished Gregor Bottoms could have seen the tryouts. He wondered if he would have made the team if Bottoms had still been the coach.

Johnny dressed quickly and walked to the parking lot. He spotted George Madison sitting alone on the curb with his head sunk between his shoulders. Johnny sat down next to him and put his arm around him, but George pushed it off.

"What's wrong, George?" Johnny asked.

"What do you mean?" asked George.

"You made the team, didn't you?"

"No."

"I didn't know."

"Coach Strauss said if I would've beaten you in one-on-one that he would've kept me and cut you."

"Are you serious? I don't believe it."

"That's what he said just now."

"What a lousy thing to do."

"I know. I was just having fun with you. I didn't know it was for keeps."

"What a rotten way to pick a team."

"I wish I would've known the game was for keeps," George said.

"Can you imagine what the game would've been like if we'd known it was for keeps?"

"We'd both be in the hospital, or you would be," George said.

"That's a pretty stupid way to pick a team, eh?"

"Yeah, it is."

George's mother drove up, and George shook his head at her. He opened the passenger side door, threw his bag onto the back seat and got in beside her. Johnny watched the car pull away. He knew what that car ride was all about. He thought of the lucky shot he had made to win the game. He thought of Rob Koch. Johnny wished Rob had gone out for the team. He would have liked for Rob to experience getting cut.

Johnny drove himself home. He had his license now. When he was home, he yelled for his mom and dad to tell them the news. He went through the kitchen and then checked the living room. He ran upstairs and checked the bedroom. They were gone. He showered and then warmed up some leftovers from the refrigerator. He ate and then left to put in four hours at the drugstore.

After his shift, he came home and found his parents in the living room. He told them he had made the basketball team. His mother smiled enthusiastically. She put her hands together under her chin like a cheerleader and looked over at his father. His father stood up, stepped over to him and held out his hand. He shook his hand like one adult to another.

"Congratulations," his father said. "Get me a basketball schedule when it comes out."

"You bet."

That night, Johnny lay in bed and thought about the fluke shot he had made to beat George Madison. He thought of his mother's enthusiastic smile when she heard the news and the way his father had stood up, walked over to him and shaken his hand; a handshake he didn't quite understand, but knew was good. It was probably the highest form of compliment his father could give.

Then he thought, *So this is it? This is all you get for making the team? I thought I would be so happy. Last year when I was cut it hurt so bad. Why am I not dancing on the roof right now?*

He heard his dad downstairs walking toward the front of the house and stop at the foot of the stairs that led to the bedrooms.

"Johnny," his dad yelled.

"Yeah," Johnny said.

"Here's what you do tomorrow. You listening?"

"Yeah."

"You go see Gregor Bottoms and you tell him you made the team. You tell him George Madison was cut and that Rob Koch didn't even try out. And then you say you're aware of his little ploy with Rob Koch, and that you're glad his plan didn't work out."

"Wow. That would be something," Johnny said.

"You do that, OK?"

"OK."

He heard his mom get up and join his dad at the foot of the stairs.

"You tell him your mother and father know all about it, too. You tell him we were very upset. OK?"

"OK."

That made Johnny happy. *Yes*, he thought, *I'm going to tell Bottoms he made a mistake when he cut me. And that Coach Strauss has corrected his error.*

The next day at school, Johnny went to Gregor Bottoms' sociology class after the lunch bell had rung. That way, there would be plenty of time for the two of them to have it out. He was worried about confronting an adult and a teacher, and telling him how wrong he had been.

When Johnny entered the empty classroom, the chair behind the desk up front was vacant. He looked the room over and spotted Bottoms in one of the back corners closing a file cabinet.

Bottoms turned and said: "Johnny! Congratulations! I heard the good news." He started toward him. "You know, son, if I were still the coach I would have kept you this year, too. Know why? Because you went out and played in the city league. I saw you play many times. I went to the tournament. You worked on your game and for that I would have rewarded you. You showed you have a good attitude and that you're not a quitter. You're a fighter."

"Thank you, sir," Johnny said. He hesitated briefly before walking out.

He wanted to tell Bottoms he had made a mistake cutting him the previous year. He wanted him to know that he knew why he had kept Rob Koch. But Bottoms had been so complimentary. He was practically slobbering on him. He didn't trust Bottoms' sentiment. What he had said was good, but it sounded too much like flattery. Still, he couldn't bring himself to denounce him. It didn't seem right. It just didn't seem right.

Chapter IX

The sun was out during the last two weeks of October, but its warmth could not be felt because the breeze was so cold. During my lunch break I would drive past the Henry Clay estate and turn into the old-money neighborhood, where the streets were tree-lined and piles of red, yellow and brown leaves covered the curbs.

Barrow Road was isolated – you had to drive a one-lane road to reach it, and it led to a dead end. I would turn my truck around at the dead end, kill the engine and coast to a stop between the same two houses every time. Leaves crackled under the tires. There I ate my lunch and looked out at the green lawns and at the black Volvos, Mercedes and BMWs parked on the blacktop driveways.

The only signs of life I would see would be the mailman, who would walk past me on the left and then turn around and walk past me again on the right, and the black collarless cat that hunted the birds that sang high up in the trees. The cat would stop with one paw in the air and look up at the branches. I would look all over the trees for a bird, trying to follow the chirping with my eyes, but I could never spot one. After admiring the neighborhood, I would pull out a book.

One day I was reading a book by Turgenev when a shiny black Mercedes sedan approached and pulled alongside my dirty, junky, dull blue truck. The driver's-side window started its descent. First I saw the blond-gray hair pulled back away from the face. Then came the dark, oversized sunglasses. She wore bright red lipstick.

The window disappeared into the door. Her tanned skin was unnaturally brown, like shoe polish. The cheeks and neck were wrinkled and leathery-look-

ing. She could have been as young as forty-three or as old as sixty-seven.

She smiled at me and laughed. "May I ask who you are?"

"I'm Nicholas." I said it as though our families knew each other and that having given her my name her memory would be triggered.

"Oh, OK," she said. "What are you doing here?"

"I'm reading. I'm on my lunch break. I come here because it's so peaceful and quiet."

"Oh, OK. We were just wondering. Everyone is very watchful in this neighborhood."

"If it's a problem, I can go somewhere else."

"Oh, no, that's fine. We were just wondering. We've seen you parked here the last couple of weeks."

"Yeah, this is a nice street. I hope you don't mind. Are you sure it's OK?"

"I don't care," she said, rather unconvincingly. She checked her rear-view mirror, then her door mirror and pulled away. She drove one house down and turned into a driveway.

I tried hard to get back into the book I was reading, but it was no use. The words did not connect. My mind was agitated and elsewhere. I looked at the houses on both sides of the street. I knew this was the last time I would ever stop here.

MEAN CLOUD

My desk is in the middle of the newsroom, which gives me a good view of all the departments and offices at both ends. In the morning, when the newsroom is calm and everyone is planning their day, I like to watch what goes on and listen as much as I can.

Every morning, Mr. Hindmarsh, the editor, walks up and down the newsroom to meet with reporters, section editors and other important staff. Some reporters act very nervous when Mr. Hindmarsh stops at the end of their desks. Some read from their notebooks to make sure what they are repeating is accurate. They tell only what they know and are careful not to talk themselves into any corners.

Then there are the confident reporters and columnists, who never read from their notes. Sometimes they try a joke or get bug-eyed relating a bizarre tale. When the story or joke is over, Mr. Hindmarsh smiles politely and either nods or replies out of the corner of his mouth. He never seems moved by what he hears. I watch this every morning.

Sometimes I imagine myself holding an important position at the newspaper one day; one that would require Mr. Hindmarsh to check in with me regularly. I even hold imaginary conversations with him. During these conversations I always have interesting things to say and he always looks impressed.

When I was offered this job, I remember being excited because I had been out of school for two months and couldn't find work. I memorized every part of the job so that once I had learned it well enough, I would be moved on to another, more important, position.

However, my boss never once mentioned anything about a promotion. I was so grateful just to be working at the paper that I felt sick with dread at the thought of asking for one. Finally, when I got up enough nerve to, I was told to be patient. That was a relief. I didn't mind waiting.

There was another matter, far away from the newspaper, that kept me worried when I wasn't thinking about work. This matter involved my good home. It was busting up and that was upsetting, because at one time it had been very beautiful and had been the best thing going for me. I thought I would always have my good home.

Even before I had a job I had a good home, and I remember thinking at the time how everyone should have at least one good thing going for them. If I had to choose between a good job and a good home I would choose a good home. After the newspaper hired me, there was a short period when I had both. Then, without notice, everything at home turned ugly. It took a long time to convince me that things were as bad as they were, and once I realized how bad it had become, I tried not to think about it because it made me so nervous and worried.

Last night, I was the only one home and it felt strange to get into bed and not have my wife next to me. I awoke in the middle of the night and was still alone. My wife had decided not to come home at all. It was the first time she had ever stayed away all night. It was difficult not to think about where she was sleeping and who she was with. I tried to go back to sleep but couldn't, so I got up. At the kitchen table I ate an apple and read the newspaper. I tried not to worry.

When I got to work that morning and sat down at my desk, Mr. Hindmarsh was at one end of the building standing outside his office. He still had his hat on, which meant he hadn't made it into his office yet. My boss approached him and asked if he had given any more thought to what they had discussed the previous day.

I heard Mr. Hindmarsh say that the position of news assistant was not a stepping stone to a reporting position. My boss countered that there were several reporters on staff who had started out as news assistants. Mr. Hindmarsh said that while this might be true, it had happened before he was editor. They both looked my way and the conversation ended. I was far enough away that they could assume I hadn't heard what was said.

I was so upset I started to tremble. They had been talking about me. I had been bugging my boss about becoming a reporter and he had gone to bat for me. It was clear now that there wasn't going to be a promotion. There were no plans for me here. I had been doing the same job for two years and Mr. Hindmarsh didn't even know my name. He nodded my way occasionally, but we had never said a word to each other. The position I held now felt demeaning and permanent.

I tried to keep all bad thoughts out and start working on something productive. Being productive would keep my mind occupied. It was no use. I couldn't concentrate. Out of the corner of my eye, I spotted Mr. Hindmarsh speaking with various staff, and then he headed my way. If he were to say something to me, I would have to make a good impression, to show him I could be useful. But he walked past me without looking my way.

After making his rounds, he stepped into his office at the end of the newsroom and closed the door. The reporters settled down to their work. All morning I slumped forward on my desk and watched the office come alive with the day's business. I felt excluded from it.

At noon, I grabbed my umbrella and took off. I didn't want to come back after lunch. I didn't know where I would go, but I knew that I didn't want to come back here. But as soon as I thought it, I knew that I would be back.

Outside the building, across Midland Avenue, the bright sun reflected off the chrome on the cars in a used car lot. The sky had cleared somewhat after the early morning clouds and rain. The sun popped in and out from behind puffy white clouds. In the center of the used car lot, two men stood over a bright yellow Cadillac. It looked new. One man got in and tried repeatedly to get it started. It wouldn't start.

I tried to think of somewhere to go. I didn't want to go home but I didn't feel like sitting anywhere for an hour. There was one place I should go. That was to the courthouse to file for a divorce. Now would be the right time; there was no denying that.

The courthouse was six blocks from the office in the heart of downtown. At this time of day, the courthouse square would be clogged with cars and there would be no place to park. Now that the rain appeared to have passed, walking would be better.

After tossing the umbrella into the car, I crossed Midland Avenue to Short Street. No one was walking along either side of the street, and no one was in Thoroughbred Park or outside the loading dock of the office supply store. At the next corner was the Christian church, and no one was there either. Past the church was a government office, and no one was waiting outside the door. It was strange to feel so alone in the city.

On the block leading up to the courthouse square, where a number of little shops and the big banks reside, cars in all four lanes were stopped dead in traffic. The sidewalk was jammed with people so that you had to be careful not to run into anyone. Most of the people were in groups, and everyone was wearing nice-looking suits. They seemed very important and busy and prepared and going places and on their way. It seemed like an exciting world they were living in. But I wasn't part of that world. I liked the walk better when no one was around and I had the sidewalk and the street to myself.

The circuit clerk's office was on the fourth floor of the courthouse. I knew no one would use the stairs, so I headed for the stairwell. My shoes scratched and scraped the steps, creating an echo. The only sound in the stairwell for the four flights up was the echo of my shoes. I thought, *You're going to make yourself sick if all you ever hear are your own footsteps.*

In the clerk's office, there was a plump woman with red hair behind a high counter, and she smiled when I came in. She had the round shoulders of middle age, and she wore her hair short so she didn't have to fuss with it. When I told her the purpose of my visit, she looked disappointed and said, "Oh, my. Well, let me see. We keep the petitions right under here."

I wanted to say something so she wouldn't feel so bad.

She pointed behind me to an adjoining room where I could sit down and fill out the petition. It was a small room made narrow by the oak cubicles along one wall and the rolling file cabinets along another.

At the far end of the room there was a man who was older than me, in his late thirties probably, who sat backwards in his chair. He had his back to the cubicles and he faced the opening in the file cabinet. He was smiling and nodding his head at a young woman who was walking back and forth between the cabinet and the files stacked on a cart. I sat at a cubicle near them. I planned to listen to them talking so I wouldn't have to think about the petition I was filling out.

"You should come down here more," the young woman said.

"Yeah?" the man answered, smiling.

"I don't have anyone to talk to."

"Really? All right, I will."

"Remember Michael?"

"Your boyfriend?"

"He was never my boyfriend."

"He wasn't?"

"Oh, no. Not at all. It never got serious. At least, I didn't think of him that way. He was just a friend; someone to hang out with."

"Oh."

"Well, listen to this. We were going out quite a lot there for a while. Then for no reason he stopped calling. He didn't call or come by for two weeks. So I called him up to see what was going on. I asked him where he'd been and why he hadn't called or come by or anything. He said he'd been busy. I told him friends didn't go two weeks without speaking to each other. Then he said that he had planned on calling. I asked him when. He said he didn't know. Well, I told him not to bother. He didn't say anything after that and I didn't say anything, so we sort of hung up."

"Oh, man!"

"It's no big deal to me, though. The only reason I called him, you know, was because I just wondered what had happened, that's all. I didn't care if he called me or not."

He shook his head dramatically. "Oh, man."

The petition was simple enough to fill out. I was filling in the names when the young woman started again: "We haven't talked since I hung up on him. It's been three days now."

"Do you think you'll see him again?"

"Oh, I hope not."

"Really?" The man gave a wide, enthusiastic smile. He had dark circles around his eyes like a raccoon, and whenever he smiled like that his eyes looked goofy. He wore a nice khaki suit and there was a briefcase at his feet. He was probably a well-respected lawyer, but whenever he acted excited he looked goofy.

There was a pause in the conversation. The man just sat there, still smiling goofily at the young woman in the cabinet. He looked at the floor and said, "Well, I'm glad it's over. You know, for your sake. And. And ..."

"What?"

"I don't know." He looked at the floor.

There was the sound of wheels rolling and the stab of high-heeled shoes on the tiled floor. I could only see the young woman from the waist up. Her blond hair had been straightened and was pulled into a tight ponytail that reached the middle of her back. She had an attractive, carefree face.

The man asked her: "Are you seeing anyone right now?"

"No."

"No? No one?" He looked excited.

"Nope. Are you?"

"No. No one at all."

He watched her going about her work. She avoided his gaze as she flipped through the files on the cart.

"Well," she said, disappearing into the cabinet.

He looked to be thinking of a response but nothing came. When she turned around and looked at him, he offered that goofy smile again.

There was a squeak of rubber-soled shoes behind me, announcing the arrival of the clerk from the other room. She was carrying a long white box.

"Who's that for?" the young woman asked.

"Who else, dear?"

"For me?" She covered her mouth with a brown folder. She took the box and pulled the front flap across. "Oh my God! Roses! Oh my God! Where's the card? Oh, here it is. Oh, this better not be from ... Yep, it is. It's from Michael." She smirked and tried her best to sound put out.

The clerk winked at me as she made her way back to the other room.

The man sat there, still smiling away. He shook his head along with her when she announced who it was from. He kept smiling as she turned the card over a second time and read the name again.

"This is stupid," she said, glancing at the man in the chair. "These are going in the garbage."

"Are you going to throw them away? Really?"

"Yes," she said. She walked past me carrying the box.

He stood up as though he planned to follow her out, then sat back down. His mouth hung open a little as he watched her walk out.

With her out of the room, the man turned around to sit in the chair the right way, reclining in it. He appeared to be having a conversation in his head. He was probably talking to the young woman, imagining her saying pretty things to him. Most likely what she would really say was, "I'm sorry, but I just don't feel the same way about you."

Then he would remember how foolishly he had acted in front of her; the constant smiling and exaggerated excitement. He would want to kick himself for acting like that.

I went back to my petition, then glanced at him again. He was stretching his legs and the familiar smile was fixed on his face. He did not look worried about the possibility of defeat. He didn't look concerned. Maybe only the defeated worry about the possibility of defeat.

After signing my name at the bottom of the petition, I went into the front office and set the paper on the counter. The clerk stopped typing and came up to me. She held the petition far away from her to read it, and her lips moved as she looked it over.

"Oh, Mr. Partin. I'm sorry." She sounded hurt on my behalf.

"No, don't be. It's really for the best."

"Oh, honey, truly I'm sorry. It's truly a shame."

I thanked her and waved goodbye.

Out in the hallway next to the stairwell, the door to the janitor's closet was open and the young woman was in there. I could hear running water filling a container. Then the water shut off and I could hear the young woman talking. She was on the phone.

The sweet smell of her perfume mixed with the scent of roses and old rotten mops. In the sink was a vase filled halfway with water, the white box containing the roses resting against the far corner.

"I can't believe you," the young woman said. "Michael, you're so sweet. You really are."

She pinned the phone between her shoulder and ear, then bent over and picked up the roses. The box fell to the floor. She set the roses in the vase and spread them out. Some of the rose petals and green leaves fell into the sink.

I opened the door to the stairwell, then paused.

"Oh, I love you, Michael. I love you so much. When are you coming to see me?"

I started down the stairs and thought about the man back at the clerk's office. He had gotten his hopes up right in front of her. It was foolish. She would never have caught me acting like that. No one would, ever again.

As I walked along the square amid the crowd, sprinkles began to dot the sidewalk. Raindrops landed on my head, and suddenly the rain turned into a downpour. Everyone in the square scattered, seeking cover. A low, dark cloud had moved in and my umbrella was back at the car. I wanted to find a rock and throw it at the cloud.

Chapter X

Three men walked into the massage parlor at ten thirty at night to find a fat woman with pretty eyes and large breasts seated behind a desk. Two smaller women, who would pass for semi-attractive, were seated beside her. The fat one looked like a talk show host, with the two women as her guests.

The fat woman looked at the men standing by the door and noticed their dirty softball uniforms. "Well, did you-all win?" she asked.

"Won two and lost two," Leo said, stepping forward to be the leader while the other two stayed back and let him. "We would have gotten here earlier if we hadn't won so much. How much for a massage?"

"For you, honey, forty dollars," the fat one said, smiling sweetly.

Leo huddled with the other two. "All right, boys, I've got fifty. Cecil, how much you got?"

"Hot damn," Cecil said. "I got thirty-five. But you can cover me, Leo."

"Derek?"

"Shit, I'm broke. I spent all my money on beer and food."

"Well, if I had enough for all of us, you know I'd take care of it," Leo said.

"I know," Derek said. "I just wish you would have told me to bring more money."

"Well," Leo said, looking at Derek. "What do you want to do? Do you want us to leave? We can leave if you want."

"No," Derek said. "You two go ahead. I'll sit out here with big Bertha."

"Yippee!" Cecil yelled. He ran over and grabbed one of the women from her chair, threw his money on the desk and disappeared through a side door.

The other woman stood up and, after Leo had paid, walked through the same side door with Leo in tow.

"Well, it looks like you're stuck with me, kid," the fat woman said. "Have a seat."

Derek sat down in the chair next to the desk and looked the woman over. He couldn't tell where the breasts ended and the belly began. It was one big mound.

"You'll have to come up sometime and let me give you the special treatment." She laughed as she spoke and her body shook all over. Her yellow teeth showed when she smiled.

Derek could hear the table legs on the other side of the wall scraping against the floor in a rhythmic way.

"I bet your girls have never even seen a man's back before, let alone massaged it."

"What are you talking about?" the fat woman said, sounding irritated.

"You heard me."

"They've got professional masseuse degrees hanging on the wall back there."

"I bet that ain't all that's hanging from the wall."

"Listen here, kid. I run a respectable joint. What are you, a cop or something?"

"No."

"Well then, lighten up." The fat woman opened a drawer, took out a magazine and threw it in his lap. It was Town & Country.

Sitting in a massage parlor in a strip mall with an intersection out the window and another strip mall across the street, in a crummy little town in Oklahoma, Derek leafed through the pictures of well-manicured lawns and gardens from an estate in the Northeast that the magazine had chosen to profile.

"I love that house," the fat woman said, leaning over Derek's shoulder. "Wouldn't it be something to live like that? Even for a day."

After about twenty minutes, Leo opened the door and stuck his head out. "Derek, take this and get as much beer as you can with it." Leo handed him five dollars and Cecil's car keys.

"Damn, Leo," Derek said. "I should have brought more money."

Later that night, when Derek finally crawled into bed, he patted the mound of covers next to him and began stroking his wife's head.

"You're lucky, Janie, you've got a good husband," Derek said, feeling proud of his fidelity.

"A good husband wouldn't wake his wife up when she's sound asleep," she said, bringing him back to reality.

IN GOOD TIMES AND IN BAD

To help settle the nerves late at night after work, it was always good to stop at Angelo's for a quickie. There I could sit in the dark with some other late-nighters and just make out their faces in the light cast from the television behind the bar. There wasn't a lot of talk, and I could go there and think about what had happened earlier in the evening.

If there were no loud talkers and if no one was talking to me, I could hear the horn that had sounded hours before, signaling the end of the ball-game. Students had spilled onto the basketball court, creating a mob scene under the basket. I had grabbed a coach and a player to quote, returned to my portable, typed as fast as I could think and filed my story to the news-paper. Then I checked my watch and basked in the euphoria that comes with beating a deadline.

After a couple of beers at Angelo's, my nerves would be settled and then I could go home. I tell you, it's wonderful when you have a job where you watch ballgames, bust your hump to beat a deadline, then celebrate your own triumph. But then, after the celebration, you're pretty much like everybody else until the next ballgame.

The duplex where my wife, Carolyn, and I lived would be dark on both sides by the time I got home, and inside it would feel quiet and empty. In bed, after I was settled in, I would sometimes hear sniffling. I would roll over and hug Carolyn and ask her what was wrong. In a shaky voice, she would reply, "We never see each other anymore."

With her working days and me working nights, we didn't see each other much. She had quit college, moved out of her parents' home and followed me to my new job in a small town in Texas. She told me she would go anywhere in the world with me. It really meant a lot to hear her say that. When we left home, we tried to make everything exciting, like it was an adventure, but nothing turned out to be very exciting or adventurous.

Our families in Kentucky were too far away for a weekend visit, and when I got home from work late at night she told me many times that our arrangement was no good: that we were barely making a living; that she missed her home; that she missed her family. I promised things would get better, but when she asked how, I was unable to provide proof. Still, I promised her things would get better.

I tried to cheer her up by mentioning the times we spent together, like when we went on walks through the hilly subdivision near our duplex, picking out our favorite houses. Each time we went out we would turn at a different street and find even better homes on nicer lawns. Or I would remind her of the times we went to church together. During the service she would get down on the kneelers and rest her elbows on top of the pew. One hand would cover the other, coiled up in a fist. She would bow her head, lean forward, pressing her lips to a finger and close her eyes. I could imagine what she was praying for: to get the hell out of Texas.

After eight months, I still hadn't made things better. Nothing had changed, except that at night there was no more sniffling; she was always asleep when I came in. She seemed resigned to the situation, and I thought maybe that was the first stage of acceptance.

Then, one afternoon, Carolyn came home earlier than normal. She rushed into the house with a smile so wide you could see her back teeth. I set down the book I was reading.

She didn't know where to start. "OK, OK," she said, calming herself. "Listen to this."

She had just gotten off the phone with her father. She said he could get me a job at a warehouse back home that paid more than I was making now. The work would be weekdays, eight to five, with the weekends off. She had also spoken to her former boss, who said she could have her old job back, selling advertising. With our combined income we would make enough money to buy a house. And best of all, she said, we would be back home again.

"What do you think?" she asked me.

I told her I didn't know; that I would have to think about it. I'll admit, the news was exciting, especially for her. She was so happy, it was hard not to get caught up in it.

She hopped into the kitchen and danced with herself, and then hopped into the living room and grabbed my hand, but I jerked it away because I didn't feel like acting the fool. She couldn't stop jumping up and down. Then suddenly the cross that we kept on the mantel fell to the floor.

It was so good to see Carolyn happy like that. It really bothered me to see her upset all the time, crying in bed and me not being able to do anything about it. I liked being a sportswriter, but the pay was so bad it was insulting. I wasn't as bothered about the low pay myself, but to expect someone else to accept it might be asking too much.

Of course, it wouldn't always be this bad. After I had gained some experience, I would naturally move on to bigger and better newspapers. But it's hard to see the future when the present is so dire. We were using every bit of both paychecks just to eat and keep a roof over our heads. We couldn't put any money away. So when the opportunity came to make more money and return home, I'll admit that I was ready to chuck journalism if it meant Carolyn being happy.

Carolyn spent the next week punching numbers into a calculator and jotting down the figures on a notepad. One evening when I came home late, she was still on the sofa, waiting to go over the plan with me. She had planned our grand return. The next day we talked it over again, and she was so happy she was in tears. I agreed to it, and we each handed in our notices at work. We were set to leave at the end of the month.

On the day we packed our belongings, Carolyn turned up the music in the house and started dancing again. I walked past her carrying a box to the truck. When I came back in for another load she started hopping up and down. She grabbed my hands and swung me around. Now I was dancing and jumping up and down, and then we both looked at the cross on the mantel and watched it teetering. We stopped jumping, but it was too late. The cross fell to the floor again, and this time it broke.

‖

Carolyn's parents offered to let us stay with them until we had saved enough money to put down a deposit for a house of our own. In the evenings, her parents would drive us to where the new subdivisions were being developed. We saw the new ranch houses going up. We never could have bought a new house with what we were bringing in before.

One Friday evening, shortly after we had moved back, I got off work at the warehouse at five. I stood just inside the warehouse door and watched the rain pelt the men as they ran to their cars. I wondered how the rest of the night and weekend would go. Every night and every weekend was spent with Carolyn and her parents. It grew monotonous, and I'm sure they were sick of looking at my mug all the time too. Dinner, help with dishes, sit in the living room with her old man and watch an old war movie. Time for bed. Can't fool around because the bed squeaks. Now Carolyn was happy and I was miserable.

On the drive home, a strong wind blew the rain sideways, making it difficult to see the road. A handful of cars had pulled over to wait for the storm to pass. I decided to wait out the storm in a bar downtown.

The place where I stopped was a dive. With the storm getting worse every minute, the bar was packed and everyone in there was wet. I took a stool and checked my wallet to see how long I could stay. The wallet was empty. We were pouring all of our money into savings then and I had already blown through my weekly budget. *Cheer up*, I thought, *that's more money saved toward the new house.*

There was nothing left to do but go home. Carolyn's old man would fix me a drink. But drinking at home doesn't have the same effect. You cannot think there. That's the difference. I needed to sit somewhere, have a drink and think. Then drink some more and think some more.

I called the bartender over. "Say, can I start a tab?"

"Sure. Just give me a credit card."

"Why do you need a credit card?"

"In case you skip out or forget to pay."

"I can't carry a tab for a week or a month or six months or a year?"

"No, sir."

Damn, I thought. Angelo let all of the newspaper guys run up a tab. That got dangerous, though, because I had let mine creep over a hundred dollars. It had taken me months to pay it down.

I ordered a draft without giving him a credit card. The bartender was busy and forgot to ask for money for the beer. I looked around the joint. It was shoulder to shoulder in every direction. Everybody was talking except me, which was fine, because I had come there to think. So I looked straight ahead at the different liquor bottles before the mirror at the back wall and tried to think.

As I sipped the beer, I recalled how, after covering a ball game, my first drink of draft was always a long chug. It was like watering a dusty infield on a baseball diamond. That first long swig helped to start the process of settling my overwrought nerves. Now that I was sitting around in a warehouse all day, opening the large doors, signing for shipments, finding space for the shipment to be stored for a week or a month, then sitting around waiting for the next load, my brain never got agitated.

So I just sipped at the beer. It seemed flat and didn't taste as good, and the coldness didn't mean anything because I needed to be worn to a frazzle and stimulated and stressed out and exultant over making a deadline. Work hard, play hard. I wasn't working hard, so it was no fun to play hard. These days, work involved too much nothingness, yet I got paid more for doing little piddling tasks than I had when I was busting my rump trying to accurately, entertainingly and swiftly report the goings-on at a ballgame.

I looked to my left at the bar. A man and a woman sitting there seemed caught up in their own conversation. To my right, two couples were fully engaged in themselves. The women were talking to each other and the men were looking at their phones. It would be nice to have someone to talk to, but I was content to focus on my own worries.

From my stool I looked out the front window at the rainwater pouring from the metal awning in sheets, slapping the pavement. The rain reminded me of all the times I got caught in storms covering ballgames. On those days I would run as fast as I could to the press box or the fieldhouse. When I finally reached cover, I would be dripping wet, but my portable and all my notebooks would be dry and tucked safely in the backpack, ready for work.

It's funny. When I was a sportswriter, I didn't care how wet or cold or hot it got as long as my tools were dry and safe. Now I get irritated at the first sign of a storm or on excessively hot or windy days.

At this time of the year, high school football was cranking up. If I were in Texas, I would be in my car driving to some little town, looking for the football field from the road. I would climb the bleachers and then carve out a little corner in the crummy press box to set up. I used to like getting everything set up early so that I had a half-hour before kickoff to watch the bleachers fill up and think about each team's strategy.

My reminiscing was interrupted by someone in the bar who yelled, "Hey, Do Nothing!"

I hadn't heard that since high school. That's what I used to be called; it was a play on my last name, Doolin. At first it had been "Do Little" but then it had devolved into "Do Nothing."

"Do Nothing! Hey, James Doolin!" I turned around to see who could possibly be calling my name in this shithole. Between ladies' shoulders and a man's arm I could just make out two men sitting at a table against the wall. I got up and walked over to them.

"Carey!" I said, shaking his hand. He was a slender fellow with a goatee, and he wore a trilby hat. I had known Carey since kindergarten.

"Say, Bruce!" I turned and shook hands with my old pal from junior high days. Bruce had gained weight. He had always been a string bean. Now, just five years out of high school, he had become a watermelon.

"Boy, it's good to see you guys," I said.

"Amen, brother," Carey said. "Sit down."

"The man from Texas," Bruce said, moving his chair closer to the wall to make room.

"What are you drinking?" Bruce asked, looking at the draft I had set down on the round table. "This is my fourth beer," he added, holding up a green bottle that was half full.

"I asked for the cheapest beer they had because I don't have any cash," I said. "Figured I'd cut them some slack when I walk out on the bill."

"I'll cover you," Carey said.

I nodded a thank-you to Carey and then turned to Bruce. "You're a married man. Why aren't you home?"

He raised his eyebrows. "Kim's having a slumber party with her niece over at her sister's house."

"I was joking."

"She thinks I'm home."

"Yeah?"

"I sneak out every chance I get."

"What have you been up to?" I asked Carey.

"Just started at Ford. Been there two weeks."

"Oh, that's great. I hear they pay really well."

"Yeah, but they work you to death. In fact, I've got to be at work at eight in the morning. I'm working just about every day now." Carey was staring into the distance at nothing. You could tell he had something more to say.

"How's the band doing?" I asked. "Still playing?"

"No, not really. No one has the time to any more. I'm the only one who gives a damn, and even I can't find the time because of work."

All three of us grew quiet and then took a drink.

Carey turned to me. "Glad to be back in Kentucky?"

"Sure."

"Good. Why are you back, anyway?"

"I found a job that pays a little more."

"Yeah? What are you doing?"

"I'm working at Young's Warehouse."

"I heard Carolyn's old man got you that job," Bruce said.

"That's true. He did."

"I thought you were a newspaper man," Carey said.

"I was. I loved it, but it didn't work out."

"What do you mean it didn't work out?"

"Well, Carolyn was pretty homesick."

Carey looked at Bruce.

"And we were broke all the time."

"Who says you were broke?" Carey asked.

"We were, Carey. Really."

"Yeah, OK."

"What?"

"Nothing. I just hate to hear anyone quit something they enjoy doing. Especially over money. Money don't mean dick."

"I know. I try not to think about it."

"You went to school too, James."

"I know."

"Man, you must be just sick about it."

"I'm all right."

"You're going to be miserable. Believe me. You're going to hate yourself. Then you're going to hate Carolyn."

"I'll be all right."

Carey went to the bar and brought back three shots of bourbon. It had a good bite to it. You could feel something happening to your head; unlike the beer, which was like drinking water.

Bruce and Carey stood up. They grabbed their coats and said they were meeting some friends at a place called The Cornerstone. They said it was good to see me again, and Carey wished me luck.

I asked if I could tag along with them.

"Why?" Carey asked. "Why do you want to come with us?"

"So I don't have to go home."

"But you don't have any money," Bruce said.

"I know."

Bruce and Carey looked at each other for a moment. "Come on," Bruce said. "But you better pay me back. Don't you still owe me money from high school?"

Carey punched me in the arm. "Not a good move, Do Nothing," he said. "Your old lady's gonna be upset."

"Do you want to call her?" Bruce asked.

"No, it's cool. I'll see her later." I turned off my phone so it wouldn't be going crazy on me.

"Your poor old lady," said Carey. "You've been such a good boy, too. Until now."

"Ah, shut up, would ya?" I said, and they both laughed.

III

The next morning I woke up on a couch in Carey's apartment. Next to me in a recliner was Bruce. His dirty-socked feet dangled near my face. *Oh no*, I thought. *What am I doing here?*

My throbbing head was a good clue. I went to the bathroom with my head pounding, and then my stomach climbed up into my throat. I leaned down and vomited into my own piss. Piss and toilet water splashed up into my face. There wasn't much vomit coming up, so I began dry heaving. I splashed cold water on my face and gargled, then went back into the living room.

On the way back I saw that the door to Carey's room was closed. I lay back down on the couch. Bruce's eyes were open.

"Anyone in there with him?" I asked, nodding at the room behind me.

"One of the girls from last night."

"What the hell happened, anyway?" I asked. "I don't remember a thing."

"We started drinking tequila shots."

"Tequila? I can't drink the stuff. I guess I was so glad I wasn't going home that I lost my head."

"You passed out in your chair. Everyone thought you were dead. You were sitting up but your head was down like this." Bruce put his head down between his shoulders.

"Me and Carey had to drag you to the car. We watched for cops while we dragged you a little way at a time. It looked like we were getting rid of a body."

Bruce started laughing in the recliner while I found my shoes and put them on. Bruce asked for the time. My watch read ten minutes past eight.

"Hell, Carey should be at work," Bruce said. He got up and knocked on the door to Carey's room. There was no answer. "I guess he'll call in sick again."

Bruce reached under the coffee table for his boots. He said he needed to hurry home before his wife got there.

"Oh, James, I almost forgot. I called your parents last night after you passed out. I didn't want them to worry. Your dad said he'd call your in-laws this morning."

"I'd better go," I said. I got up and walked to the front door. "See ya, Bruce. Thanks for taking care of my sorry ass."

"You owe me twenty dollars. And you owe Carey ten."

"I won't forget."

The sun was blinding as it reflected off the gravel walkway and the pavement of the parking lot. The streets were wet in the center but were drying out along the edges.

It was nine o'clock by the time I turned into my in-laws' subdivision. I saw my father-in-law's truck crest a hill and approach me. I stopped and waved for him to stop. He rolled down his window and looked down at me with sunglasses covering his eyes. His cheeks were white and puffy, and there was no expression on his face. He pulled alongside my car, peered into my face with a look of intense anger, and then rolled on by. My heart was thumping.

I pulled into the driveway, hurried through the garage and then stepped into the kitchen. Carolyn's mother was standing in front of the stove with a cup of coffee and a crutch under each arm. She saw me come in and raised her eyebrows.

"You're in deep shit, boy," she said.

"What happened to you?" I asked, bewildered by the crutches she was leaning on.

"That's not your concern right now. You'd better go talk to Carolyn. She's upstairs getting dressed for a wedding."

I ran through the house and up the steps. I called out, "Carolyn, Carolyn." There was no response.

I opened the door to her parents' room and found her sitting at her mother's vanity. I could see her face in the mirror. She refused to look at me. The skin below her neck was red and blotchy. Her neckline always broke out when she was upset. She lifted a tiny brush to her right eye and patted her lids, then set the brush down in a plastic case, making a clicking noise.

In a calm and steady voice, she said she had called every hospital and police department in Lexington and Nicholasville. She had phoned all of them late the previous night and had just started calling again in the morning when my father called.

"Since you wouldn't answer my repeated calls or texts, I thought something had happened," she said.

She stood up from her chair and came over to me. Her lips were trembling. She balled up her fists and started swinging and landing blows. I couldn't duck fast enough. Finally, I gave up ducking and just stood there and took it. She tired quickly and tried to catch her breath. I thought she was going to pass out. I steadied her so she wouldn't fall onto her parents' bed.

She slapped my hands away, then started to cry. "Is this what you want? Is this what you want?"

My stomach was churning again. My throat opened up, but I clenched my mouth shut, holding the vomit in. The upstairs bathroom was being remodeled. The only working bathroom was downstairs. I didn't want to leave Carolyn while she was so upset, so I just stood there with vomit filling up in my mouth.

"You don't care about me! You don't care about us!" She was talking so fast she had to pause to catch her breath. "I didn't know you were like this. If I'd known you were like this I never would have married you.

"Do you ever think of me?" she continued.

I looked away from her. My cheeks were about to pop.

"Why can't you answer me?"

I couldn't bring myself to look at her. I was afraid I would blow chunks all over her parents' bedroom. I was sure I would feel good about our circumstances eventually. She wouldn't have to worry. We would be all right. I wouldn't carry on like this.

When the reply she was waiting for didn't come, she said, "We're not going to be very happy, are we?"

Chapter XI

Bryant figured the defense would stiffen at the goal line if they ran the ball. Tobe would have a tough time scoring. The safeties had stepped up to the line, clogging the holes.

Bryant spent the team's last timeout. The crowd sighed and sounded a little put out that their hero had delayed the game-winning touchdown they were anticipating. He looked into the stands on the way to the sideline. Cigarette smoke drifted above the heads, mingling with the smell of popcorn and coffee. The crowd drank coffee because the air had turned chilly now that it was dark.

Bryant told Coach Carlisle that the defense had read their play. He suggested a pass. Coach Carlisle's craggy face reddened. If the coach had had a stick, Bryant bet he would have broken it over his helmet.

"You listen to me, goddammit! I haven't won six championships because I listened to you. Now give the goddamn ball to Tobe and let him punch it in! We've got time for two plays, and Tobe's going to score on one of them."

There were six seconds left on the clock. Bryant doubted he could get two plays off, especially if one of them was a run. As he ran back to the huddle, Bryant signaled for everyone to listen up. "OK, we're going with Tobe up the gut on two. Let's go."

Tobe's eyes widened. Just don't fumble, he thought.

As the offense approached the line, Bryant grabbed Fry, the split end, and said, "Don't block your man. Roll to the corner of the end zone."

"But ..." Fry said.

"Shut up and do it!" Bryant shouted.

Coach Carlisle spit when he saw Bryant talking to Fry. What the hell,

Bryant? he thought to himself. *Fry knows the play. He knows who to block. You don't have to remind him.*

Bryant stood over center. The defense formed a straight line, bunched up close in the middle, waiting to pounce.

"Red 35, Red 35, hut, hut."

Bryant took the snap, stepped back, tucked the football behind his right leg, then threw his left hand into Tobe's gut.

"What the hell?!" Tobe screamed, stopping suddenly.

Bryant rolled to the left and waited for Fry to turn around. He was alone in the back corner of the end zone. Bryant flipped a soft, lazy pass into Fry's arms. Fry secured the ball into his lap and fell on his back. The crowd hesitated as the referee slowly raised both arms.

The roar that followed sounded like a train in a tunnel; it shook the field. Then came individual screams, whistles and cow bells clanging.

"I knew it would work," Bryant said, running into the end zone. He was the first to jump on Fry.

Coach Carlisle looked at the clock. There was one second left. He cursed and spit on the ground again.

After kicking the extra point, the home team led by six. On the kickoff, the visitors tried a few pitch-backs, hoping for a miracle, but they were tackled to end the game. The crowd rushed onto the field to celebrate the team's first undefeated regular season. The players continued the celebration all the way to the fieldhouse. After a while, the boys ran out of steam and the celebrations subsided.

Coach Carlisle walked in quietly, looking as if they had lost, then called Bryant into his office. Bryant went in and closed the door behind him. He stopped in front of the coach's desk. He knew what was coming.

"Son, you played a whale of a game," Coach Carlisle said, leaning back in his squeaky chair, his shoes pushing against the edge of the desk. Then he tossed his hat across the room in disgust. "But I have never in my twenty years of coaching football been treated with as much disrespect as you showed me out there tonight. I wouldn't say this to you if it was the last game of the year. I'd tell you to go rot and that would be it. But we've got the playoffs coming up and I want you to tell me right now who's in charge.

"If you want to be in charge, that's fine. I'm quitting and so are all of *the coaches, because I hired them. I'd love to go home after school and live a normal life. But I don't because I think there are lessons to be taught out there on that field. And I enjoy teaching them. It makes me feel good to teach young people. But every now and then some kid comes along who thinks he knows more than me. I've never been confronted by one of those kids myself; I've only heard other coaches talk about them. Tell me, are you one of those that knows more than me?"*

"No, sir."

"Who's going to run this team, me or you?"

"You, sir."

Carlisle jumped to his feet and slammed his fist down on the desk. The loud thud of bones crushing on wood startled Bryant. He was suddenly aware how hard the coach could hit.

"Then why in the hell did you switch plays after I told you to hand the ball off to Tobe?!" Carlisle's face and the whites of his eyes were a deep red.

Spit sprayed Bryant's face. He didn't dare wipe it off. "You told me earlier in the year that I could audible if I saw something I didn't like." Bryant's voice quivered. Dammit, man, be strong, he thought.

"What did you see?!"

"The linebackers and safeties were on the line, looking at Tobe."

"So what?! Tobe would've rammed the ball in for the score in two plays and it would've run the clock out. Instead, we give them the ball back and they have a shot at scoring and winning the damn game."

"You're right, coach."

"If you cost this team a championship, I swear to you I'll rip your balls off and serve 'em to the team. And believe me, they'll eat 'em if I tell 'em to. Now get the hell outta here!"

Bryant reached for the door and opened it, letting in the sound of the last few revelers. He undressed and walked to the shower area to get into the whirlpool. Several of his teammates patted his shoulder, congratulating him.

Bryant leaned back in the hot, swirling water, the jets massaging his sore muscles. "Great audible, Bryant," he told himself. "Thanks," he said in reply.

DISPLACEMENT ON THE INTERSTATE

On the sidewalk in downtown Dallas, in the warm shade of a tall office building, a young man loosened his tie and unbuttoned his collar. His coat was folded over the briefcase on the ground. It was late afternoon in the summer, and it was very hot in the street. The humidity made his shirt stick to his chest.

He took out a handkerchief and dabbed the sweat from his face. He liked that he always kept a handkerchief on him. The man stood near the building, out of the way of the sidewalk traffic, and whistled to himself. He enjoyed the time right after work.

He felt a flutter of excitement when he saw the silver four-door pulling to the curb, barking its tires to a stop. He gathered his briefcase and coat as a young woman got out of the driver's side wearing a sharp-looking navy-blue suit. She high-stepped quickly around the front of the car without any shoes on. It was like walking across burning coals.

"I hate this weather," she said. Sweat matted down her bangs and the strands around her ears.

"You drive," he said.

"No. I hate driving."

"Where are your shoes?" he asked.

"I hate them, too." She got in on the passenger side and slammed the door.

Oh, no, the man thought. *Not the pissy attitude. Please, no.*

He put his things in the back seat, then went around the back of the car and got in to drive. The good, tired warmth he had felt was ruined by the arctic blast blowing from the car's air conditioner. Cold air always made his bones ache.

He turned the fan down to low, but the woman flipped the switch back to full blast, almost ripping the knob off in the process.

"In a bad mood?" he asked.

"Aren't I always?"

Yes, he thought. He looked in his side mirrors and started to pull into traffic. The woman turned to look out the back window.

"No! No! No!" she yelled.

He mashed the brakes, jarring them both forward. "I wasn't going to go. I saw it," he lied. The car in question beeped as it went by.

"You can go now if you punch it," she said.

"Why don't *you* drive?"

"I'm trying to relax."

He pulled out too slowly in front of a delivery truck, forcing it to swerve into another lane to avoid a collision. The truck driver honked his horn and stayed on it while he passed.

The woman braced herself on the dash. "Ugh," she said. "You don't know how to drive, do you?"

"Ah, hell. He was going way too fast. I wish he'd lost control and rammed into the side of a building." He waited for a response. None came. He looked over at the woman, whose mind was already somewhere else. "What happened today? What's got you in this mood?"

"Nothing. It's not just one thing; it's everything. I hate my job, all right? You know that."

"It's just work, honey. You go in, do your job, then go home. That's all there is to it."

"Yeah, you can say that. You don't get bitched at like I do."

"Sure I do. I just don't tell you about it."

"Oh, listen to you. You've got it easy. Try working for someone who treats every little thing like it's life or death. Every day when I go in I pray there's not some new crisis."

"Everyone has it rough. You just don't know how to manage it."

"Listen to you!"

"Well?"

"Well, maybe I don't want to manage it. Maybe I'm sick of it all. Maybe I don't want to live like this any more."

They were approaching a line of cars stopped in all six lanes of traffic. He pulled up as far as he could without hitting the back of a pale blue Cadillac. The traffic didn't budge.

"Come on!" He punched the horn angrily.

"Look at you," she said. "Why are you so mad?"

He chose not to reply.

"It's just traffic, dear," she said, using her husky voice. "Everyone's suffering out here."

He remained silent.

"I'll be glad when you get your car back," she said tauntingly. "I don't like riding together. You're a reckless driver. I bet that's how you got in that wreck. You've got a bad temper and you're careless."

"Are you trying to start a fight?" he asked.

This time she chose not to say anything.

"Is that what you're trying to do?" He looked over at her. She was wiping tears from her cheeks and eyes. All the anger that had been building up suddenly went out of him.

"Why do you let work bother you?" he asked.

"I don't know. I wish it didn't. I wish I didn't care. I wish I was like you. But they don't know how to treat people. They try to make you feel like you're incompetent or a ditz. I hate it. I hate my job."

"It's so simple and you make it so hard. Just go to work, do your best and then go home. Do the best to *your* satisfaction. Not anyone else's. Just yours. That's it. Once you're satisfied, then that's it. Let it go. You can't accommodate everyone."

"Did you ever stop to think that maybe I'm no good at this?"

"But you *are* good. You're *very* good. You're one of the best. You always reach your goals. You're the best. You just worry too much."

"Well, I hate it. I've always hated it. I don't want to do it any more."

"You're talking stupid."

"Now you're going to call me names?"

"You want to quit? Is that what you're saying?"

"Yes."

"Bullshit! Don't let them do this to you. If you quit you'll only make them happy. Do you want them to be happy?"

"*I* want to be happy. Don't you want me to be happy? You used to say we were a team."

"We are a team."

"I wouldn't want you to do something you didn't want to do."

"I don't want them to run you off like that. I want you to kick their asses. Show them you can handle all their shit."

"I want to do something else. I don't want to live like this any more."

"No. Don't let them win."

"I don't care. I don't want to live like this any more."

"But you can kick their asses. You know you can."

"But I hate it. How many times do I have to say it? I hate sales!"

"Ah, toughen up. Nothing out there is easy."

She started crying more steadily. She was choked up and struggled to speak.

"Look at you. Those piss-ant bosses of yours. They would laugh right now if they could see you. If I felt the way you did I'd knock their fucking teeth out. But look at you. What do you do? You cry and blubber about it."

"I hate you!"

"Tell them to go to hell."

"*You* go to hell!"

"If you talked to them the way you talk to me you'd be the sales manager by now."

The traffic still hadn't budged. Everywhere they looked they saw cars and trucks and the same gray and black office buildings. Birds flew playfully from building to building, then disappeared. The sun was almost down behind the buildings by this point. Their time off was ticking away, wasted in traffic.

"C'mon!" The man yelled at no one in particular, riding the horn again.

He inched closer to the back end of the Cadillac. The driver shot up his middle finger in the rear-view mirror.

"What the …?" the man said. "Did that bastard just flip me the bird?"

"I hope so," the woman said.

He pressed on the horn. The Cadillac driver threw up another bird.

"What the hell is he doing?"

"Yeah!" the woman shouted. "Show him another. Give him both middle fingers. Show him your middle toe if you can."

The man rolled down his window and stuck his head out. The Cadillac driver saw the man's head outside the window so he did the same. He was so fat he struggled to turn all the way around to face the man behind him.

"Why the hell are you flipping me off?"

"What?" said the fat man, stretching his neck out as far as it could go.

"Open your fucking ears, fat man!"

The fat man heard that and ducked back inside. He extended his stubby arm outside the window and, in full view of everyone downtown, exposed his chubby middle finger in a sustained gesture that lasted a full five seconds. The fingers next to the middle one were squeezed tight in his palm to give the offensive finger even more height and stature.

"He's giving me the bald eagle. That commie cocksucker."

The woman applauded. She was impressed.

The man opened the car door and put a foot out, but as he did so the traffic began to move. He got back in, shifted into drive and began tailgating the Cadillac.

"I'll kill that son of a bitch."

The traffic was moving faster now and the Cadillac wedged its way over to the far left lane. The man followed. The Cadillac's left turn signal blinked, indicating that he would be turning onto the interstate. The man, whose way home was straight, put his turn signal on to follow.

"What are you doing?" the woman asked.

"I'm following Mr. Bird. I'm gonna break those fucking fingers." He was grinding his teeth.

"This is my car. You're not going to wreck my car, too. Take me home."

"Shut up! For once in your life just sit back and shut your trap!"

The Cadillac was a rust bucket from the seventies. Whenever it accelerated, stinky black smoke poured out of the tailpipe. It merged with the interstate traffic and moved to the left lane. The man stayed to the right and sped up until he was level with the Cadillac.

He rolled down his window. "Why are you flipping me off?!" he shouted, on account of the wind.

The fat man was unable to roll down the passenger window because of a short in the power. He attempted to signal this, but it was lost in translation. The fat man started laughing. He was shaking all over when he saw that the man didn't understand his signals.

The man began gesturing to the Cadillac driver about his obesity, making a semicircle above his chest with his hand. "What's your problem, fat man?" he said in the voice of a halfwit. "Why you, why you, why you so fat? Huh? Why you so fat?"

"You're an idiot," the woman said.

The man swerved to the left, as if to smash into the Cadillac, then jerked it back into the right lane. The fat man grabbed the steering wheel with both hands. Gone was the wide grin and the playful look in his eyes. The situation had become very serious.

He slowed his speed, but there was a red Porsche tailgating him, flashing its headlights. The fat man shouted at the man, drew out his middle finger again and then sped up.

"That bastard flipped me off again."

"Let him go!" the woman said. "You're going to get us killed!"

"No way. You don't flip four birds and get away with it."

The man moved into the left lane behind the Porsche and the Cadillac. When the Cadillac moved into the right lane, the man followed. The Cadillac's left blinker came on but the car swerved right at the last second and got off on the ramp at the Plano exit. The man followed with expertise.

A half-dozen cars were stopped at the bottom of the Plano exit, waiting at a red light. The Cadillac pulled up behind the last car on the ramp and stopped. The man pulled in right behind it. Then he opened the door and got out.

"What are you doing?!" the woman screamed.

She watched him get out and walk up to the Cadillac. The fat man was looking in the side mirror, so he saw the door of the car behind him swing open. He watched the pair of legs walking toward him, getting closer and closer. He rolled up the window and locked the door.

The man grabbed the door handle and pulled hard on it. When the door didn't open, he began pounding on the window.

"Open the door!"

"No!" the fat man was bug-eyed.

"I'm gonna break your fingers."

"No you're not."

"Get out here. Take your beating like a man."

The light changed and the traffic began to move on the exit ramp. The fat man saw this, floored the gas pedal and took off.

"Coward!" the man screamed, kicking the back end.

His car pulled up with the woman behind the wheel. She didn't look at him or even slow down. "What are you doing?!" he yelled.

He watched the car turn left at the light and disappear under a viaduct.

Cars on the Plano exit blew their horns as they swung out wide to avoid hitting him. He looked around and assessed the situation. He spotted a service station with a bench out front.

This is just like her, he thought. *She finally gets indignant and takes a stand but she takes a stand against the wrong party: me. She's such a wacko.* He began talking as if she were next to him: "Why don't you stand up to your bosses like this? Huh? Huh?!"

He made it to the shoulder of the exit ramp and headed for the service station. *I guess I'll wait a while for her to calm down and then call her to come pick me up.*

In the car, the woman had turned left twice and was back on the interstate.

He is such an ass, she thought. *He's going to get himself killed. I see how he deals with stress. Well, I don't want to be like that. I'm not going to be like that. I'll never be like that.*

I'll let him calm down and then pick him up when he calls. What a wacko he is. She spoke to him as if he were sitting in the passenger's seat. "I can't keep living like this. I'm quitting sales. That's it! I hate it! As soon as I find something else, I'm quitting. Do you hear me?! I'm quitting!"

Chapter XII

Nate was sitting in chapel during holy hour one Sunday when he decided that the core of his being – the reason he existed, the only thing that really separated him from other people – was his intense interest in the small details of life. Little nuggets of human experience that every person has and likes to share with others interested him the most.

He enjoyed pulling those experiences out of people and decided that from that day forward, he would be more conscious of it and practice it more until it became a skill. It could certainly help him as a serious writer, which was what he wanted to be.

The next day, he went to Louisville on a trifling newspaper assignment. He stopped at his grandfather's house beforehand for a short visit. He thought, OK, your grandpa has a wealth of knowledge and experience, having lived through two world wars and the Depression. Listen and remember.

They sat on the front porch as the sun dried the dew on the small, rectangular yard and talked about hunting and fishing. He learned that the reason night fishing with a lantern was so effective was that the flies were attracted to the light and the minnows came after the flies and the fish came after the minnows.

"To become a sharpshooter," his grandfather said, "you should lift the heel of your back foot so that your weight is forward, and be sure to concentrate on squeezing the trigger."

Then his grandpa talked about a half-blind woman who had lived across the street from him years earlier. She had called the house one day and asked Grandma to send Grandpa over to change a light bulb. Grandpa had changed the bulb, and when he came down the ladder the woman had put her arms around him and kissed him like he had never been kissed before. He said his peter got stiff, and he was excited and surprised at the same time.

"You know, a stiff peter has no conscience," he said.

Grandpa then went on to talk about another woman he knew and said he couldn't understand how she could have left her grandchild the way she had without saying goodbye. She had strained relations with her son and his wife, and one day she had simply picked up and moved out of state. Her grandson loved his grandmother and she him, but she had chosen to leave and never see any of them ever again.

"But before you leave, I want to tell you something," Grandpa said. "You can't think for someone else. I don't know what's going through her mind to up and leave like that. But I do know you can't think for someone else. You know what I'm saying? You remember that."

Nate told him the one thing he would remember from this conversation was that a stiff peter has no conscience.

He looked at Nate. "Now don't get carried away with that."

MRS. DUMONT AND THE AROUSED TENANT

Mrs. Dumont entered the dining room and walked around the head of the long table just as her tenant, Woodrow Mourning, crossed at the other end. She nodded good morning then stopped, her mouth agape, as she peered at the young man's midsection.

Her look also made him stop. She placed her hands on top of a chair and caressed the wood. The man placed his hands, one on top of the other, in front of his privates.

"Woodrow," Mrs. Dumont chirped. "What is that projecting from your trousers? Is that an erection?"

"Ma'am?" Woodrow said, aghast. "Uh, no, ma'am. These pants, you see, have a wrinkle that …" He tried to smooth the material so that it lay flat, but to no avail.

"Woodrow, don't you think I know the difference between a wrinkle and an erection?"

"Well …"

"My boy, what is stirring such an arousal? Every time you enter the parlor, I fear you're going to knock something over."

"Well, ma'am, it could be the cool breeze that blows in through the window or the smell of your biscuits baking in the oven."

"Nonsense. Out with it, dear boy. What makes you so excitable? You're a young man, sure enough, but I don't see other young men walking about like that."

"Ma'am, this subject is very embarrassing. I don't wish to discuss it, if you please."

"You're my tenant. Perhaps there's a problem. I could suggest a doctor, vapor therapy, a lozenge, or perhaps a cold cream."

"No, ma'am. A doctor won't be necessary. These things come and go."

"Beg pardon, but yours does not. You walk around like a circus tent every morning, noon and night. It's like a pointer."

"Ma'am, forgive me, but you exaggerate. It doesn't happen that often."

"My boy. The salute is constant and never failing, as my dearly beloved Edgar said on our honeymoon."

"Th-that's an insult to my intelligence. Shouldn't I know when and how often I salute better than you, with all due respect?"

"Well, Woodrow, rare is the moment that I see you when you're not at attention. It frightens my poor Muffy."

"That is malicious and hurtful, your grace. I'm afraid your poor Muffy is a tad skittish, if I may be so blunt."

"My Muffy is not skittish, dear boy. My Muffy has been known to take on all comers, great and small. She holds her own and then some. You would be wise to hold your tongue around my Muffy. You'll keep all thoughts on that subject to yourself, if you know what's good for you."

"Well, I most certainly will refrain from any future interaction with your Muffy. And I pray I will keep all thoughts of your Muffy to myself, my lady."

"That is wise of you, dear boy. But my Muffy is not the only one who's afraid to be in your presence. The neighbors have started to call before they visit. My parlor has always been open to the street, but now no one dares drop in if they think you might be lurking about with that flagpole."

"Your neighbors and callers are always very kind and polite whenever I make their acquaintance. This is news to me."

"Haven't you noticed that they don't linger when you're here, dear boy?"

"That's because they have other engagements, my lady."

"Nonsense. They scurry and scatter like frightened birds in your presence. Your bulges could snarl traffic. They see that log in the road and are afraid they'll trip on it, or worse, get trapped underneath it and have to call the fire department to get extricated. Your protuberance, my boy, is a road hazard, if you please. I need to set orange cones round you and hang signs from your neck that read 'Hard hat area' or 'Road closed to thru traffic.

Detour.' Would you be opposed to such a tactic? It would be most helpful to friends and relatives of this manor."

"Dear lady, I'm getting rather steamed up by this conversation, if the mistress of the house would forgive me."

"Will getting steamed up lower the mast, dear boy?"

"No, my lady. But if I may have permission to lay my pipe in the cleavage of your fatty baguettes, and then agitate it in the peaks and valleys of those lovely dumplings, that should be sufficient to make it burst. Then said pipe would retract to a more agreeable size, God be praised."

"Well I never! What vulgarity!"

"You wanted to know the cause of my arousal. I must confess it is your abundant baguettes, dear lady. Your milk ducts are large and round and a creamy white, like ivory and ..."

"But I'm old enough to be your grandmother."

"A ripe cucumber knows no age and has no conscience, my pink and wrinkled rose. Cupcakes covered in satin and lace are ageless."

"You debaucher! You hedonist! How dare you?"

"You broached the subject, pretty as you please. Now, if you want this red hydrant emptied you must pump it repeatedly until it has flooded the floors. You must exhaust its contents completely. Well, what will it be?"

"Out! Out! Oh! Oh! What impertinence!"

"You wish for me to take it out? Very well."

"Oh! Oh! The beast is among us!"

"Shall I place it between your baguettes or would you like me to aim higher? Well? What shall it be? We mustn't tarry. We must strike while the iron is hot, as they say."

Mrs. Dumont's eyes widened and her jaw dropped, one hand resting on her cheek.

"Ah-ha! I see you've decided on a destination. Splendid. I'll just pop it in and you can vanquish it like you would a cream horn. Here we go."

Woodrow unbuttoned the top of his pantaloons, but stopped at the sound of Mrs. Dumont's shriek.

"Out! Out! I'll not be accosted by some depraved bohemian." Mrs. Dumont was frozen to the spot.

"Very well. This is one cock that shall not crow on this day of our Lord.

Good day, Mrs. Dumont. I'll take my considerable package elsewhere."

Woodrow exited the dining room, passed through the parlor and opened the front door. He looked back at Mrs. Dumont. "By the way, I'll be moving out, if you please. And so as not to frighten your poor Muffy or any of your neighbors or relatives, I will make arrangements for someone to come and get my belongings. Good day."

"By all means," Mrs. Dumont said. "But I don't want you to go off at half cock."

"You don't want me to stay at full cock and you don't want me to go at half cock. We're running out of options, my lady. Good day."

Mrs. Dumont watched as her aroused tenant struggled to exit the house. At first he tried to leave sideways, but the opening proved too narrow for his temporary extension. He stepped back, turned carefully and walked straight out. When he turned back to close the door behind him, his midsection bonked into the side of the door, making the rapping sound of a wooden knocker.

"Come in. Oh," Mrs. Dumont said, realizing the noise came from Woodrow, who was still occupied in taking his leave.

What insolence. If he were a real man he would have taken me instead of threatening me. The very thought of that offensive appendage being thrust between my heaving, convulsing whatnots and gouging forbidden zones!

Mrs. Dumont felt herself moistening. "The very thought indeed," she whispered, fanning herself. She drifted upstairs to change her undergarments.

Chapter XIII

The sea receded into the base of a rising swell. Nate felt the tug pulling him out. The swell grew into a wall, rising and rising until there was only wall and sky. Just when he thought it couldn't get any higher the wall curled into a roll and began to topple over with white froth, like the head on a beer.

He turned his body into a missile and leaped out in front of the breaker. The crash came and tossed him like an empty bottle. He succumbed gladly to the torrent. The sea's strength and muscle pounded from every side. He was at its mercy. He was certain he could be snapped in two and wondered if this was how it would end.

The sea spat him onto the shore with elbows and knees dug into the sand. When he stood up, he was disoriented. He did not recognize the umbrellas poking into the beach at a slant. The sea had carried him farther down the coastline. He shook water from his hair like a wet dog. His eyes were bloodshot and his throat ached with thirst. He returned to the sea, eager for more; again and again, over and over.

NINE DAYS TILL CHRISTMAS

He was an old man, and if you were to ask him why he went out at night and drank so much, he would tell you it was the crowd and the way they crammed into a bar called Kaleidoscopes that kept him coming back and staying out as long as he did. He lived downtown and would walk there once or twice a week.

By the time he was just a few paces from the front door, he could hear the crowd inside the bar. Someone would open the door, and then out would come a tremendous roar. The racket people made when they were enjoying themselves always got to him.

One evening late in the year, a cold wind blew through the damp streets, bending the limbs of the trees and stripping them of their old leaves. The old man put on his heavy coat and descended the three flights of stairs inside his apartment building. He took each step carefully, stopping to catch his breath on the landings.

Once outside, he crossed the street and cut through the church court-yard, where he stepped awkwardly on the cobblestone and turned his knee. He bent over to catch his breath and feel his knee to see if it was hurt. It was twisted, all right. He limped to the front gate of the courtyard, hobbled across the four lanes of Main Street and went one block down to where Kaleidoscopes stood on the corner of Upper and Vine.

Inside, it was crowded and loud as people talked over one another. Women twisted their heads in conversation. Men opened their mouths as wide as they could to bark out a laugh. There were always people crammed into the booths along the wall or at the tables in the center of the room, but at least one stool would be available at the bar because people normally came to sit in groups.

Kaleidoscopes was an upscale college bar, and everyone there dressed nicely, so the old man dressed as well as he could: a clean flannel shirt, khakis and a sheepskin coat. The students could tell he wasn't a bum. They passed enough bums on the street around Kaleidoscopes.

The old man sat on a stool between two groups that had formed separate huddles at the bar. Neither group acknowledged him. The girl behind the bar was new and looked a lot like the clientele, so when he sat down, he noticed that she also ignored him. She had long, straight, blond hair and her large, round breasts projected proudly from inside her white turtleneck. She was at one end of the bar talking to a young chap.

The old man made eye contact with her, but she didn't budge. Finally, he rapped on the bar and she came over out of a reluctant sense of duty.

"Aren't you going to ask what I want?" he asked her.

She didn't respond. She just stood before him, unsmiling.

"You're new, but you fit right in," he said. "I am always treated this way here."

She took a rag and wiped a spot on the bar. She appeared bored.

"Get me whatever's on tap."

We have, like, eight different beers on tap, ding dong, she thought to herself.

When she brought him the beer, he said, "When this stein is empty, that means I want a shot of Beam. Seven-year-old."

She thought, *Stein? Who are you, Kaiser Wilhelm?*

She returned to the end of the bar and the young chap.

The old man noted that the bartender had not uttered a syllable to him. Not 'Here you go' or 'Enjoy' or 'Go F yourself.' Nothing.

He held the cold glass in his hand. The first taste was always the best. He wasn't going to let the bartender ruin the first swig. He swallowed the tingly cold beer, then turned around in the stool to look over the crowded joint and consider each member.

The table closest to him caught his attention because a loudmouth was standing up, holding court. He wore a bow tie, had a bushy, unkempt beard and was top-heavy. *He can't talk to just one person,* the old man thought. *He has to jabber to everyone within earshot.*

The loudmouth was supposed to be in a one-on-one conversation with a fellow seated at his elbow, but whenever he spoke, he looked at everyone around the table. *He wants everyone to admire his witticisms. Every generation has its loudmouths.*

The old man recognized the loudmouth as a regular at Kaleidoscopes. He was always with the same girl: a brunette with short hair. She was sitting at the table, looking up at her boyfriend. *She looks very decent and very bored and extremely put out by her boyfriend's outrageous behavior. But she won't dump him because he's the life of the party and she needs to be with a fun crowd more than she needs to be happy.*

You've got to hand it to the loudmouth, though. He knows how to handle himself in a crowd. He has confidence. He will never find himself alone in a bar, like me. He could approach a stranger and start a conversation because he has enough confidence for both of them. His only problem is that he can't tell when his charm becomes annoyance. They are the same to him. If he came to talk to me, I would recommend that he watch people's faces closely. The face will show if he's still entertaining or has crossed over into obnoxiousness.

Next to the loudmouth's table was the all-male table, made up of engineers or math majors or scientists of some sort. *They want to meet girls, but that would involve leaving the comfort of the pack and opening themselves up to the possibility of a public rejection. It's easier to sit and watch the girls go by. I would like to introduce the loudmouth to that table. He could give them tips on how to come out of their shells.*

The old man would start with the tables and work his way to the booths, trying to figure out the personalities, problems and desires of each person. It was an interesting exercise. After he had determined someone's destiny, he would turn around and take a drink. What he really wished was that someone, anyone, would strike up a conversation with him so he could learn about them instead of having to guess.

What's the matter with these people? he thought for the thousandth time. *You know, it wouldn't kill them to talk to me. Hell, when I was their age I used to seek out the oldest gentleman in the bar and strike up a conversation. They were always the most interesting to me. I guess I was different that way. But it was true, how interesting the old timers were, because they had lived so long and had seen so much.*

Like the time I sat down next to an old horse trainer years ago. He talked about how he would wake up at four in the morning to go to work and how he would drink in the afternoon and then go to bed. He had been retired for twenty years but he kept the same routine because that was what he was used to. He could sleep in as late as he wanted, yet his eyes opened at the same time and he would get up and go to the farm and watch others prepare the horses.

If he was too old to do the work himself, he felt like he was still part of the operation by watching it. Horses were his life in the morning, beer and bourbon were the afternoon, and sleeping was the rest, was how he had told it all those years ago.

The old man looked around at all the pretty girls and studied the newest styles in clothing and hair. The girls seemed to get prettier every day. *Years ago, there were so many ugly women, a pretty one stood out. Now it seems everyone is beautiful and well-built.* He missed the eye play he used to make with girls. He could almost always pick up a girl at a bar like this when he was younger. He missed that very much.

He remembered all the times he would be sitting with some worthless characters talking rot, and then he would spot a girl at the bar. When his companions left, he would go over to the girl and they would talk, and he would either give her a lift home so she wouldn't have to pay for a cab or just keep her company while she was there so she wouldn't be alone. It was all so long ago, but he remembered.

He didn't like the boys in the bars now. They were so smug and arrogant and ruthless. Their open disrespect for girls was disgraceful. *A boy will turn his back on his girlfriend to talk to a friend or another girl and not even introduce her. She'll sit there alone while her boyfriend chats away, ignoring her entirely. But the girls don't protest. In my day, you couldn't treat a girl the way they're treated now.*

One thing is true now that was true in the old days: girls have no interest in old men. When he was young he never saw a girl go up to an older gentleman and strike up a conversation. It just did not happen. He would like very much to hear what interested the young girls of today, but he knew it would be impossible to find out. The boys surprised him. He expected that someday a boy would want to chat, but it hadn't happened in all the years he had been going to Kaleidoscopes.

On this particular night, the old man had drunk four steins and four shots of bourbon and could feel the pleasant effects of both. He motioned the bartender over and placed a wad of bills in her hand.

"This is for you, daughter," he said.

He tipped her well, hoping he could buy her friendship. She didn't acknowledge the gesture. She put the money owed to the bar in the register and dropped the rest into a pitcher full of other tips, then returned to the young chap at the other side of the bar.

I'd better leave before that bartender talks my ear off. If I tipped her by the word, she'd get nothing.

When the old man got up and made his way over to the door, the young chap at the end of the bar asked the bartender, "Why does an old man like that drink here at a college bar?"

"Old men like that are disgusting," she said. "I know what's going through that dirty mind of his."

"Look! Oh, I thought he was going to fall down."

"Filthy drunk," she said as she watched the old man limp out of the bar. She checked the window next to the front door to follow his movements in the street. She watched him take a right and head for Main Street. "I bet I can set him up with someone tonight." She went over to use the phone.

Outside in the quiet of the street, the old man heard a long, sustained note playing in his head. It sounded like a violin bow pulling across a single string. A cold, sharp wind stood him up straight. The liquor, warm inside him, made the contrast exhilarating.

As he walked unsteadily up the steep part of Upper, the pain in his knee was becoming unbearable. He had wrenched it more seriously than he had thought. He listed like a ship, only in a more exaggerated way. Whenever he drank he exaggerated all of his movements. It was the only way he could feel his limbs in space. *You drink too much. You'd better take it easy now. Be steady.*

When the red light stopped the traffic, he put his head down and entered the crosswalk. He concentrated on stepping carefully across the striped pavement. In the middle of the street his knee buckled, almost pitching him to the ground, but he recovered and jogged to the other side, wincing through the pain.

He was rubbing his knee at the corner when he felt something tug at his elbow. He turned to face a tall, wide-shouldered, dark-mustached policeman in a coat and cap standing before him. The name Sheppard was stitched into his coat in gold.

"Say, old timer. Having trouble?" Officer Sheppard asked.

"Yeah, I've got a bum knee," the old man said. "But I'll make it."

The sweet, sharp, liquored breath entered the officer's nostrils, forcing him to turn away. He squeezed the old man's elbow and walked him to the wrought-iron fence of the courtyard.

"Where you headed?" Sheppard asked.

"Home."

"Home, huh? How much have you had to drink tonight?"

"That's none of your goddamn business!"

"Oh, it's none of my business. You're stumbling downtown. You smell like a distillery. That *is* my business. Where do you get off talking to me like that?"

"Listen, I'm going home. I want to go to bed."

"You're not going home. You're coming with me." The officer pulled the old man toward him.

The old man tensed up and pulled away. "Why do I have to go with you?"

"You're a nuisance," Sheppard said, reaching for him with both hands and squeezing his arm tighter this time.

"And you're an insolent bastard! I want to go home. I have the right to go home." The old man jerked his arm twice but couldn't pry it loose.

Sheppard forced him against the fence, patted him down and then led him to the car, pushing him into the back seat.

"I've never been arrested in my life. I'm eighty-six years old and have never been arrested."

"Well, you're not going to get bombed and walk around downtown."

"You can't tell me what to do."

"I'm telling you how it is."

The old man shared a holding cell with two young, shirtless men. The three of them sat on a white bench against a gray wall. The light was so bright it was offensive, and the toilet was backed up and stunk of stale urine. The two young men looked at the old man and spoke of wrongful arrests, and waited for the old man to pipe in with his. When he didn't, they urged him to but he refused to speak or look at them. He blinked repeatedly to keep from passing out.

"Come on, old man, tell us why you're in here," one of the men said. "It helps to pass the time. If we don't talk, the time drags."

"Leave him alone," the other one said. "Can't you see he doesn't want to be bothered? Old people want to be left alone."

"Not always, they don't," the old man said. "Not all old people wish to be left alone. Sometimes, yes. I wish to hell that Sheppard character would have left me alone."

The two men laughed.

"You smell like you just crawled out of a bottle," the first man said. "Were you driving?"

"No, just walking."

"What a lot of crap," the first man said. "Why arrest an old man who's out walking? Can't the cops see he's not long for this world?"

"Pedro," the other man said.

"I wish to be left alone now," the old man said. "I'm in no mood to talk. I'm upset and disappointed with myself."

At three thirty in the morning, a policeman opened the door and asked the old man if he wanted to call someone to pick him up. He said he didn't have anyone to call. At seven thirty he was released.

He stood up. His neck was stiff, his body ached and he felt extremely tired.

Sitting behind a desk, the jailer handed him his wallet and belt.

"Give me my stuff, you common thief," the old man said.

"Here you are, you common drunk," the jailer said. "You know, a man your age spending the night here with us," he shook his head, "that just don't make good sense."

"I guess I can look after myself. Have done so for eighty-six years."

When he got home, the old man felt like a stranger in the tidy apartment. The furniture looked back at him with shame. He scolded himself: *Why must you be such a stupid, goddamn drunk? So this is how you've turned out? This is what you've become?* He knew he was better than that, but the facts suggested otherwise.

Four days later he went to the courthouse for his trial date with the judge. The judge read the file and double-checked the man's age. He looked up from the file at the old man standing before him at the podium.

"What are you doing here?" the judge asked.

"People should not be treated the way I was treated the other night by your henchman," the old man said.

The judge winked at the court clerk beside him and then went back to the file. "It says here you were intoxicated and stumbling around on Main Street on Thursday night."

"I was fine. I have a bad knee, but I was fine. I was going home."

"When you're intoxicated on the street, sir, you're a danger to yourself and others who may be on that street."

"That's horseshit. That's complete horseshit. I was not a …"

"You do not address the court in that manner. You hear me? I'll have your drunk ass locked up for contempt."

The old man bit his tongue. He wanted to say that his opinion of the law enforcement in this town did not rise to the level of contempt.

For two weeks, the old man stayed away from Kaleidoscopes. He tried not to think of the place. *Cops will be watching. I'm not walking into their trap.* In the evening he would pace the sidewalk in front of the apartment building, smoking a cigar and looking into the church courtyard for the police. He looked beyond at the rush of cars on Main.

It felt good not taking a drink since the night he had spent in jail. But he knew the day would come when he would want to drink again. *It's getting bad, this town. It's getting to where you can't go out and enjoy a little self-destruction.*

It was a Thursday, nine days before Christmas, when the old man put down the book he was reading and leaned back in the recliner to think. *Well, old boy, you're a coward. I never thought I'd think of myself that way, but it's true. This is the time of day you would walk to the bar for a drink. You get yourself arrested and now you're scared to cross the street. You still cook and clean and make your bed and iron and read. You're doing everything you've always done except the drinking, and that was the best part.*

The thing is, you can't just sit at home all the time. You have to get out and see some of the world. You can't sit here and think about yourself and your own problems and worries. You need to look at someone else's face and think about their problems and their worries. At your age, having a drink out is one of the few things left for you to do.

Well, if you must go down there again you'll have to cut down on your drinking. But you've always been bad about that. You can never tell at the bar when you've had enough. You've always drunk until you were ready to go home. It had nothing to do with the number of drinks. Well, this time, let's be conscious of the amount we drink. Let's have three beers and three shots and call it a night.

He got up, put on his coat and walked to the bar. As always, the place was packed. A cacophony of clinking glasses, mumbling voices, a woman's piercing laugh and two men shouting across the room at each other was a welcome change from the monotonous silence of his apartment.

"Give me a draft!" he ordered over the three-deep crowd at the bar. All the stools were taken.

The girl behind the bar was the same blond from a few weeks ago. She ignored his order, then watched him squeeze his way through the crowd to the front of the bar.

"I want a draft. And keep 'em coming."

She turned around to fulfill his request without a reply. She put the beer down in front of him and then looked over him to take someone else's order.

"She's really something, that girl," he mumbled to the young man beside him. "She doesn't know her trade. If she's going to work behind a bar she has to make the experience pleasant for the customer. She's thinking only of herself. You can't do that in this business."

The young man did not acknowledge the old man's remarks.

The old man turned around to take a look at the crowd. Every table and booth was filled. There weren't enough chairs, so people stood around the tables and at the end of each booth. Everyone looked happy to be out. It made the old man smile to see people talking in such an ebullient manner.

I wonder if I'm the only one here who won't get laid tonight. What about the bartender? Her attitude stinks. Maybe she won't get laid either. No, she has breasts. She'll get laid tonight.

He spotted a table where a cheerful-looking couple was sitting and drinking with a man who looked sullen. They were all around the same age. The sullen man ignored the couple's attempts to lift his spirits. When he wasn't staring down at his glass, he was staring at a booth full of girls.

He doesn't like being a third wheel, the old man surmised. *He has been hurt, possibly betrayed. He doesn't trust women. He would like to trust a woman, but he's not optimistic about them and acts very moody when they're around. That's a pity. He needs to know there are good women in this world who are worthy of his trust. He'll have to be patient, though, and not give up hope. And for God's sake, drop the gloomy disposition. No one likes a gloomy doubter.*

The old man turned his attention to the booth of girls, who held such intrigue for the gloomy man. A waiter was standing before them, taking their drink orders. One of the girls ordered exactly what her friend had ordered. She was beautiful with long, dark hair and dark eyes. Her appearance was meticulous.

She looks like she sings in a church choir. She should be at a prayer meeting or a church function. She's not comfortable here, but this is where her friends want to be, so she accommodates them. She'll drink a little but has no enthusiasm for it. While the others are settling in for a long night, she'll politely excuse herself and leave. She'll be gone before the wolves begin to hunt.

She doesn't want to meet a man who spends a lot of time at a place like this. One day she'll have to stand up to her friends and cut out all of this degenerate bar business. Wouldn't it be nice if a good boy walked up to her, took her hand and said: "Come on. Let's get out of here"? That would be something to see.

The loudest table was whooping and laughing at a big-breasted woman wearing oversized gag glasses, who was circling the table, cracking jokes. All of the boys and girls loved her antics. *Her problem is, she's a friend to all but a lover to no one. She wants to be more than a pal, but she can never get anyone to consider her as anything other than a sidekick and drinking companion. She wants to get serious with someone, but she's not sure how to make that transition.*

It was another night, much like the others, except this night the bar was so crowded it took him much longer to study the members of each group and to read their histories and futures. After three beers and three bourbons the old man had barely considered half the crowd. He wasn't ready to leave. He decided to stay a little longer and drink a little more. It would be OK.

Again, no one came over to talk to him. A stool opened up, so he was able to sit and study and swivel back to face the bar to drink, and then swivel back for more study. Finally, after six beers and six shots, the old man signaled the bartender over so he could settle up. A few in the crowd watched as the old man got up to leave, but no one said a word to him.

"Goodbye, friends," the old man waved to the crowd. Those sitting closest heard him and chuckled.

The bartender watched him walk out and head toward Main. She went over to the phone to make a call.

Outside, the old man felt the sidewalk move and the buildings spin. He walked unsteadily. *You can't keep doing this. You're killing yourself. You're too old for this shit. All right, here we go. Let's hurry crossing Main and then make a run for the gate. Once I'm inside the courtyard I can rest. I just need to make it to the courtyard. I'll be safe there.*

His knee began to throb. He limped up to the intersection, then crossed Main in a half jog. With the cars stopped and their headlights on him it was like crossing a theater stage. His right side dipped low to the ground, then his left side straightened him out again. His right hip started to ache; it was giving him trouble now.

Where the hell did that come from?

He reached the courtyard and pulled the gate toward him. As he did so, he felt someone clutch his right shoulder and slam the gate shut. He turned around and it was the policeman who had arrested him previously.

"Not you again," the old man said.

The smell of liquor on the old man's breath was so pungent that Officer Sheppard turned away, coughed twice, kicked at something and then spat on the sidewalk.

"You're making it hard on yourself, old-timer," Sheppard said. "This is your doing. I told you before how things stood; that I wouldn't let you walk downtown in this condition."

The old man's head dangled between his shoulders and he was wheezing, still struggling to catch his breath. Behind him, the wrought-iron fence of the church courtyard was strung with Christmas lights. Above his head, a lighted wreath hung from the gate.

"You're not going to bully me," he said. "I have the right to go home."

Sheppard took hold of his arm and felt him tense up. "Let's go," he said. "The car's parked over here."

When the officer pulled his arm toward him, all the strength seemed to go out of the old man. He fell forward and dug his fingernails into Sheppard's coat sleeve to keep himself from falling. Sheppard stood him upright, then let go. The old man fell forward again. Sheppard caught him and kept one hand on his shoulder.

"Jeez, old-timer."

"What?"

It became apparent that Sheppard would have to carry the old man across the street to the car and then up the steps to the police station. And he was heavy as a steer.

"Listen, Sheppard. I want to go home. If you'll let me go home, I promise I'll never come out to drink again."

Sheppard remembered the sergeant asking everyone to look for opportunities for random acts of kindness during the Christmas season. Sheppard interlocked arms with the old man and felt his weight fall into him. "Come on, I'll take you. Show me the way."

"I don't need your help."

"You can't even stand up. Now point the way."

"Why can't you leave me alone?"

"Point the way!"

The old man pointed toward the courtyard gate, so Sheppard opened it. They walked arm in arm under a row of ginkgo trees along the cobblestone. Light from the moon exposed the face of a lamb made of stone that was lying among the wood chips.

The old man dropped to his knees and began coughing. He spat and then vomited. Sheppard could hear the splatter on the leaves. He patted the old man's back and helped him to his feet. The old man shook his head and spat repeatedly.

"Nice out tonight," Sheppard said. "If you weren't so sloshed you could have enjoyed the mild weather we're having."

The old man noticed that the wind lacked its cold, sharp bite. The air was warm and the heavy coat made his armpits turn moist. His forehead dripped with sweat.

They made it out of the courtyard, across the street and up the three flights to his apartment.

"Well, try and have a Merry Christmas," Sheppard said. "Do yourself a favor and sober up over the holidays."

"Listen, I appreciate the fact that you didn't throw me in the tank tonight. I thank you for that. I want you to know that I'm never going out to drink again. I might not drink again, period."

"You know, if you didn't get so smashed you wouldn't have so much trouble getting home. Do you have to get cockeyed?"

"I know I drink too much, and I'm stupid about it. But all of that is over now. I'm quitting it. No more."

"Well, that's good. That's the best thing you can do for yourself. But if I see you out in the street like this again you're going back to jail. I promise you."

"All right, all right. I'm tired and I want to go to bed. If you'll just back up."

The old man shut the door. He heard the policeman out in the hallway shout: "I'll be watching you. You hear me? I'll be watching."

He turned around and looked over his room.

"My God, this little apartment never looked so good." The newspaper was stacked neatly on the table beside the lamp. There was no trash visible and everything looked neat and tidy. He opened the door to the bedroom. "Hello, bed."

He pulled the covers back and sat on the edge of the bed to slip off his shoes. He put them in the closet, then took off his clothes and hung them up. He put on pajama bottoms but no shirt. His head was pounding. Experience told him he would be sick again in a little while. He went into the kitchen and returned with a pot, which he put on the night stand.

It was good to lift his feet off the ground and get under the covers, where the sheets were cold at first but would warm up in no time. The pillow felt good under his head, but he couldn't close his eyes because the room was spinning. Instead, he blinked repeatedly.

He couldn't stop thinking about the cop and how he had promised him he would stop going out to drink. Right now, giving up drinking was easy. He didn't want another drink for at least a hundred years. But in a week or so, he knew he would be ready to drink again. And when the time came to drink he knew he would return to Kaleidoscopes.

Only God can help me now. And that will involve forgiveness.

Maybe there's a better way home; one that will elude Sheppard. An alley or a back street. I'll go search for one tomorrow during the daytime.

Chapter XIV

Nate lined one into the outfield that rolled all the way to the bicycles parked on the sidewalk, which served as the left field fence. It was easily going to be a stand-up double. As Nate rounded first on his way to second, Jarrett blocked the base path, forcing him to swing out wide to get around him.

Jarrett waited for Nate to get close, then stuck out his foot and tripped him. Jarrett yelled for his teammate to fire the ball in. Nate scrambled to his feet and hurried toward second. He saw the ball come in to Jarrett and then felt the smack of the ball in the middle of his back.

Jarrett had thrown the ball as hard as he could from point-blank range. Jarrett was twice Nate's size and four years older. The impact of Jarrett's throw from close range felt like the sting of ten bees. Nate collapsed on the field in a heap.

"You're out," Jarrett said, laughing.

Fitz, who was watching the game from the Edwards' house, where he was drinking water from a garden hose, charged the infield like a heat-seeking missile. Not a word was spoken by Fitz. Not a protest, not a complaint; just a swift, menacing charge.

Watching Fitz closing in on him, Jarrett raised his arms to absorb the impact of this runaway train. "Fitz, Fitz," Jarrett cried pitifully.

Nate rolled over to watch.

Fitz leaped into the air, cocked his right arm and struck Jarrett on the head as he landed on top of him. Jarrett fell backward and Fitz followed him to the ground. Repeated blows struck Jarrett across the head, chest, ears, nose, neck and arms. Jarrett rolled over on his belly and covered up while the pummeling continued.

The players on the field looked at each other, not quite sure what to do. Anyone attempting to break up the beating risked having Fitz turn on him.

Finally, Mr. Baker, mowing his front yard across the street, stopped the mower and yelled for Fitz to cut it out. Fitz stopped and looked around for the person yelling and then spotted Mr. Baker standing in his yard.

"You and Nate go home! Right now!" Mr. Baker's son Bobby was also playing in the game. "You know you boys are welcome here, but not if you're going to fight. Now go on home."

Fitz thought about explaining what had happened, but then decided against it. Mr. Baker didn't look interested in arbitrating a dispute.

Fitz motioned for Nate to follow him. "Come on, let's go."

Nate walked along with Fitz through right field onto the Edwards' driveway and under the basketball goal. The other players watched them walk away.

Nate was sure Fitz was the greatest person living.

THE LAST WEEK OF SUMMER

Every summer, in the middle of the week before school started, Grandma and Grandpa Jackson would pick up their grandsons, Fitz and Nate, in Nicholasville and drive the hour-and-a-half to their home in Louisville. For three days they would fish and swim and play in the abandoned lot of the old school their father had attended as a boy. On Saturday morning, the boys would be driven back home in plenty of time to adjust to the reality of school on Monday.

When Nate was eleven and Fitz fourteen, Nate hoped the trip to Louisville would be a great adventure for them. They didn't have to be brothers for the week, fighting over territory and other trivial matters that had them at each other's throats all the time at home. They could act like best friends and partners exploring a new frontier together.

While they packed and talked about the trip in their room the night before, Nate noticed a difference in the way Fitz spoke to him. Fitz treated him like he was a confidant or a real pal, going over all the things they would do and how much fun they would have. Maybe it was because Nate was getting older. The trip had such a different feel to it; Fitz wasn't going to treat him like a little kid.

During the long drive to Louisville, Fitz and Nate tried not to think about what would be happening in Nicholasville while they were away. Their dad liked to rearrange the beds and toy chests for no good reason, and their mom would be buying new school clothes along with pencils, erasers, paper, folders, spiral notebooks and new lunchboxes. They would look at all of it laid out on the kitchen table and feel an empty sickness. On the refrigerator would be the newspaper clipping with the names of their new homeroom teachers and all their classmates. Fitz would rip the clipping off the refrigerator, ball it up into a wad and throw it away.

But all of that was a week away. This week would be all fun and play, without any parents to lord over them.

Once they reached Louisville's city limits, Fitz and Nate marveled at the amount of traffic and the cars darting in and out of lanes on the Watterson Expressway. They passed Cardinal Stadium and Purina's big soybean silos. They turned off the expressway and drove through a residential section, where the houses were small and the lawns were neatly sectioned into little rectangles.

"I bet it's great living here," Nate said, looking out the window.

"I wish we did," Fitz said.

Grandpa pulled up to the curb in front of the shotgun house and let everyone out while he drove around to the alley in back and parked the car in the detached garage.

Grandpa set the boys' fishing equipment in the garage and carried their suitcase into the small bedroom just off the kitchen. Fitz and Nate followed Grandpa into the room and sat on the bed. The room was so cramped that only one person could walk beside the bed at a time.

Fitz got up and pulled the folding door all the way open to let some light in. Nate clicked on a lamp, which gave the room a fuzzy, yellow-orange glow. This had been their dad's room when he was a boy. Not much had changed. It was like stepping into the 1940s. His old comic books were in a box under the bed along with an album of baseball box scores and articles from newspapers the year his team had won the high school state championship. The tops of the dresser and table were cluttered with Grandpa's cigar boxes, another small, circular box with a rubber lion's head for a top, tissues coming out of a woman's head and a collapsible clock that didn't work.

"You want to look at Dad's old comic books?" Nate asked.

"Nah," Fitz said.

"You want to look at his box scores and read the stories?"

"Nah, I'm going outside."

Nate followed Fitz to the front door. They could hear their grandparents changing their clothes in their bedroom.

"Grandma, can we go outside?" Nate asked.

Fitz had already opened the door.

"Sure, but stay on the front porch," she said.

Nate watched Fitz jump off the porch and continue onto the sidewalk. He stopped and looked up and down the street. Nate leaned on the handrail at the top step.

"Grandma said to stay on the front porch."

"She was talking to you," Fitz said.

"She meant both of us."

Fitz looked up the street again and stared at something. Nate looked in the same direction but couldn't see anything because the neighbor's tall rose of Sharon bush blocked his view.

"Looky what's coming down the street," Fitz said.

"What?"

"It's a little Jap boy."

"How do you know he's a Jap?"

"'Cause he looks it."

"He might be Chinese or something," Nate said.

"No, he's a Jap."

A little black-haired boy, swinging his arms wildly, walked up to the telephone pole next to where Fitz was standing and slapped it, then turned around and started walking back up the street.

"Hey, kid," Fitz called after him. The boy turned around. "Come here a minute."

The boy walked toward Fitz but kept his distance on the sidewalk.

"What's your name?" Fitz asked.

"Kim," the boy said. He began swinging his arms again.

"Kim?" Fitz looked back at Nate and made a funny face.

"Yep," the boy said.

"Where do you live?"

The boy pointed up the street toward the corner grocery.

"That's a grocery store," Fitz said.

"I live above it."

"Oh, do your parents run the store?"

"Yep."

"What country are you from?" Nate asked.

"I was born in South Korea."

"Ha, ha. Told you," Nate said to Fitz.

"Shut up, dickhead," Fitz said.

Kim laughed.

"Hey, Kim, how old are you?" Fitz asked.

Kim held up five fingers.

"I bet you could whip my brother."

"Shut up, Fitz," Nate said.

"Who, him?" Kim nodded at Nate.

"Yeah," Fitz said.

Kim shrugged his shoulders.

"He called you a little Jap when he saw you walk up," Fitz said.

"No, I didn't," Nate said to Kim. "*He* did."

"No," Fitz said. "I didn't say nothing. He called you a little Jap boy."

"Shut up, Fitz."

"Go whip his ass, Kim. He shouldn't get away with calling you names like that."

Kim followed the front walk to the porch and stopped to look up at Nate, who was leaning on the handrail. Nate was twice his size without the steps.

"Don't listen to him, Kim," Nate said. "He's just trying to start trouble."

Kim's face got red. He stared at Nate for a long time.

"He's easy to whip, Kim," Fitz said.

"Shut up, Fitz."

Kim continued to stare at Nate and Nate stared back. He noticed Kim didn't blink once.

"Spit in his face, Kim."

"Shut up, Fitz."

Kim moved his mouth a little, pursed his lips and lunged at Nate, shooting out a spray of spittle. Nate turned his head. He felt the wet spray touch his cheek and neck, and when he turned back around he could smell Kim's breath along with the spit. Kim ran to the telephone pole and hid behind it. Nate wiped his face and neck with the tail of his shirt.

"You little shit!" Nate screamed, jumping down from the porch.

Kim took off up the sidewalk but Nate caught him before he reached the corner grocery. Nate grabbed Kim by the throat and started choking him and shaking his head.

Nate screamed: "You stupid little Jap shit, cock sucking ..."

Fitz fell backwards on the grass laughing. The screen door swung open and out came Grandma. She spotted Fitz rolling around in the front yard.

"Get up here on the porch, Fitz," she yelled. "Where's Nate?"

Fitz stood up and pointed up the street. She saw that Nate had Kim in a headlock and was beating the boy's head with his fist. She heard him say, "There, you like that, you little Jap shithead?"

"Nate!"

Nate immediately recognized the voice and released the boy. The boy started throwing punches and spitting at Nate, so Nate put him in another headlock and watched Grandma hurry down the porch steps, through the front yard and turn the corner.

"Let him alone, Nate," she said. Grandma grabbed Nate's arms and freed Kim's head. Kim had tears in his eyes.

"They were calling me names," Kim cried.

"I know, I know. I heard it. Now you go on home. I'll take care of them," she said.

Kim walked backwards, crying and watching as Grandma Jackson pinched Nate's arm and led him back inside the house.

Once Fitz and Nate were inside, Grandma ordered them to bed. She closed the folding door so that it was completely dark in the room. It was eight-thirty.

The boys could hear Grandma and Grandpa talking in the kitchen. They held their breath and made no noise so they could hear the conversation. Grandpa said he was disappointed, but he thought they should still go fishing tomorrow.

Fitz called for Grandma to come into the room.

"We're sorry, Grandma," Fitz said. "We'll be good for you the rest of the week."

"OK, boys, now get some sleep. Grandpa's going to wake you up at six o'clock to go fishing."

She drew the folding door and the room fell dark again.

Nate stomped his feet under the covers. "Oh boy, we get to go fishing," he said.

"Yeah," Fitz said. "If we hurry and go to sleep, when we wake up it will be the morning."

"Bet I can go to sleep first," Nate said.

"I'm too excited. I'm not tired at all."

"Me either."

"If you hadn't of got in a fight with Kim, we could be out there watching the Reds and Dodgers with Grandpa."

"You started it."

"Ah, hellfire. I was just playing."

"Well, what would you have done if somebody spit in your face?"

"Oh, he was just a little kid."

"So?"

"I can't believe he spit in your face. What a brave little dumbass."

"If Grandma hadn't come out, I would've beaten the shit out of that little turd."

"Well, at least they're not taking away the fishing," Fitz said.

"Grandpa sounded like he was thinking about it."

"I know. Grandma kept talking about what shits we'd been with Kim and got him all upset at us, then I guess she smoothed it over. There were a couple times I couldn't hear what Grandma said."

"Grandma's the best. Mom would've killed me, then Dad would have had me buried and said good riddance."

"You know what?" Fitz said.

"What?"

"Come Saturday, Grandma won't say a word to Mom or Dad about Kim."

"Nope. She's the best," Nate said.

"I think I can go to sleep now," Fitz said.

"I'll try too."

It was early in the morning and still dark outside when Grandpa came into the boys' bedroom and tugged at their big toes.

"Who in here wants to go fishing?" Grandpa asked. He had an early-morning crankiness in his voice. "Well, I don't guess anyone here wants to go fishing."

There was no response. Fitz rolled closer to Nate and brought the covers up under his chin. Nate was under a mound of covers. Grandpa tugged at their big toes again, then picked up their feet and dropped them. They fell like corpses.

Grandpa walked out of the room, leaving the door open. He clicked on the light in the kitchen, which lit up the lower half of the bed.

Fitz lifted his head and blinked repeatedly. His head was heavy and clouded. He shook Nate. "Come on, wake up."

"No," Nate said.

"Come on. You want to go fishing, don't you?"

"Leave me alone," Nate said.

"Fine. I'm going fishing." Fitz threw the covers off both of them, crawled over Nate, digging his knee into his brother's ribs, and stepped into the kitchen. He watched Grandma carefully lay strips of bacon onto the frying pan.

Grandpa came in from the back room and saw Fitz standing there, rubbing his eyes. "There's one up," he said. "Where's your brother?"

"I don't think he's gonna go."

"All right, we'll just leave him here. What do you say?" Grandpa said to Fitz.

"OK."

"What do you say, Grandma?" Grandpa said. "We'll just leave Nate here."

"Hush," she said.

The bacon started to crackle, and soon the whole house smelled of bacon. Grandma, Grandpa and Fitz were at the table eating breakfast when Nate walked out. He appeared to be struggling with the weight of his eyelids.

"Hi, honey," Grandma said. "Care to join us?"

The next half-hour was like a military operation. Nate sat at the table eating cereal and bacon while Grandma cleared the table of dishes and handed them to Grandpa, who washed them and stacked them on the draining board. Grandma then toweled off the dishes and put them away.

Grandpa enlisted Fitz's help to pack the car with fishing equipment while Grandma made sandwiches and filled the ice chest with soft drinks. Nate was at the bottom of his cereal bowl by the time Grandpa and Fitz came back into the kitchen. Grandpa said, "OK, everything's packed, let's go."

Nate ran into the bedroom and changed out of his pajamas. He heard the screen on the back porch slam. Then he heard car doors open and close. The car engine started. Nate was dressed except for his shoes. He carried his shoes out to the car and got in the back with Fitz. Grandpa got out and checked the back door to make sure it was locked, then got back in the car.

"There's one in every crowd, isn't there, Fitz?" Grandpa said.

"Yep," Fitz said.

"I guess I made it in time," Nate said.

Grandpa drove out of Louisville and into the country to Huppman's Farm. Huppman had a five-acre lake stocked with smallmouth bass, bluegill and catfish. The lake was surrounded by woods. Beyond the woods was a hay field studded with tall, round bales. Grandpa followed the wheel ruts into the woods and parked where the bank leveled off. Down the embankment, between the tree branches and leaves, was the glittering blue lake.

"Who's going to catch the most fish today?" Grandpa asked. "Your dad used to catch more fish than me and Grandma combined. He was some fisherman, your dad."

Grandpa got Grandma set up first. She set up straight down from the car with a folding chair. She took nightcrawlers, mealworms and two pole holders to stick into the bank. Fitz and Nate grabbed their poles and followed Grandpa to the other side of the lake. It was difficult finding a clearing on the bank with all the trees, bushes and underbrush. Grandpa spotted an opening and motioned for Nate to take it. He told him to be careful casting, as the tree limbs were low, and then handed him a plastic cup of mealworms.

Grandpa put Fitz about twenty yards up from Nate, warned him about low limbs and gave him a plastic cup. Grandpa could never stay in one place. He circled the lake three times in an hour, fishing for smallmouth.

Everyone was in their spot when a splash and a thrashing of water erupted in front of Grandma. She reeled in her line. The boys studied their bobber but listened intently to what was going on with Grandma.

From God knows where, Grandpa yelled over the lake: "Got one, honey?"

"Ah, he's just a little thing," she said.

"Hey boys, Grandma caught one." Out of sight, Grandpa sounded far away.

"Way to go, Grandma," Fitz said.

"Way to go, Grandma," Nate repeated.

A little later, Nate watched his bobber go under and pop back up. The bobber moved to the right a little, circled, then went under deep. Nate reeled in a baby bluegill.

"Got one, Grandpa!" Nate screamed.

"Good boy," he said.

"Hey, Fitz, I got one."

"Did ya?" Fitz said.

As soon as Nate's line hit the water on the next cast a keeper-sized bluegill struck. He liked the bluegill's weight and the way it jerked and fought the hook.

"Got another!"

"Thatta boy, Nate!" Grandpa said.

Nate looked all around the bank for Grandpa but couldn't see him. He wanted to show him the size of the fish. He slipped the stringer through the fish's mouth and out through his gill. He tossed him in at the shoreline and buried the metal stake into the mud.

"How are you doing, Fitz?" Grandpa asked.

"OK, I guess."

"Getting any bites?"

"Yeah, a couple."

"No, you're not," Grandpa replied.

"Yeah, I've felt a couple."

"No, you haven't. You're stuck in a tree aren't you?"

"No, I'm not."

"Yes you are."

"How do you know?"

"I'm right behind you."

Fitz turned around and looked high up the hillside between the trees to the flat area up top but didn't see him. He heard Grandpa's boots coming toward him, crushing leaves and twigs. Fitz tugged at the line, but the hook was buried into one of the low-lying limbs. The branch bent toward Fitz, then Fitz let off when Grandpa walked up. He took the pole away from Fitz and jerked it hard to the left, then right.

"Stand back," he said. Fitz ran up higher on the bank.

Grandpa tugged so hard it was at the point of either the limb or the line breaking. "You got it caught real good, Fitz." He pulled harder and the branch bent more. The line snapped and the limb straightened out, making a swishing sound. The line fell limp into the water. Grandpa reeled in the line, tied on another hook and bobber, pierced a mealworm in the mid-section with the barb and made a low sideways cast that went out as far as Fitz could cast overhead.

"There, now, leave it out there." Grandpa's cranky voice had returned. He was sweating at the forehead and armpits. Fitz could smell the sweat coming through the army jacket. "Stop reeling in and casting so much. That's when you get snagged. Just leave it out there."

The sun was high up in the sky now, and a quiet heat fell over the lake and woods. Grasshoppers and other insects started making their racket. They would stop briefly and then start that long, irritating song again. Nate heard Grandpa walk up to the top of the flat area and then come back down to where he was fishing.

"Looky here, Grandpa," Nate said. He started pulling the stringer in. The bluegill made a splash, then jerked and darted sideways.

"Ooh, that's a nice one," he said. "We'll take that one home and fry him up."

Grandpa walked back up to the top to the path, then crossed directly behind Fitz and went farther down to where the lake curved. Due to the uneven ground and thick underbrush on the hillside and the fishing pole in his hand, he had no choice but to go the long way round.

Fitz studied his bobber but nothing budged it. He studied it so hard he imagined it was moving, so he jerked the pole and the bobber went under. He started reeling in, then realized what he was feeling was the weight of the worm and the hook. He decided this was a bad spot and reeled in. He picked up his cup of worms and headed toward Nate.

"Want to find a new spot?" Fitz asked.

Nate was reeling in the line. "Yeah, OK. I think I've got all the fish on this side."

Fitz considered shoving the little braggart into the lake, but the noise and commotion and Nate's bawling would alert Grandpa and Grandma, so he just waited for Nate to gather his things.

"Come on, follow me," Fitz said. He walked along the bank, dodging tree limbs. Up ahead in a little clearing, Fitz spotted a shallow dirt pit with a hole in the middle of it. He walked up to it, peered into the hole and then jumped back.

"What is it?" Nate asked.

"There's a snake curled up in there."

"Really?" Nate rushed over, then hesitated before slowly peeking into the hole.

"Oh, man," Nate said. "He's big."

Fitz looked in again. The snake didn't move.

"It's a cottonmouth," Fitz said.

"No, I think it's a water moccasin," Nate said.

"Well, see for yourself, dickface," Fitz said, shoving Nate forward. Nate leaped over the pit and landed on the other side.

"You cocksucker!" Nate screamed. The snake still didn't stir.

Fitz dropped his fishing pole and worm cup and jumped at Nate, grabbing him around the neck. Nate held onto his pole, stringer and bait, trying to fight Fitz off as best he could. Fitz squeezed his neck. Nate tried to jerk loose, but Fitz had a good grip. Nate dropped his tackle and Fitz started dragging him toward the pit. The bluegill flopped in the dirt.

"Stop it!" Nate shouted. Fitz threw a hand over his brother's mouth. The snake was coming out of the pit, showing its full length. It headed toward the water. Fitz kicked Nate's feet to keep him moving closer to the snake.

"Fitz!" Grandpa yelled, but he was too far away. "Fitz!"

Fitz let go of Nate. Nate picked up his tackle and the stringer and took off running. The snake slipped into the water and disappeared.

"You boys go to the car now!" Grandpa shouted.

"It's OK, Grandpa," Fitz said.

"No, no! You go to the car. I'll be up there in a minute."

As he ran through the densely wooded hillside, Nate kept his head down, looking for snakes. Twigs and branches smacked his head and ears, so he had to slow to a walk. He veered straight up from the embankment and stepped outside the woody growth onto the flat path. He could hear Fitz following him at a slow pace.

Nate followed the flat area around the lake to the dirt road that led to the car. When he reached the car he leaned his pole on the trunk, then set down his worm cup. He walked the bluegill, speckled with dirt, down to the bank where Grandma was monitoring two poles in the holders that were stuck in the mud. He flipped the fish into the water next to her stringer and sank the spike.

"You-all are gonna get it now," Grandma said. "What have you all been doing?"

Nate turned around and saw Fitz lean his pole on the trunk of the car next to his. He didn't answer Grandma.

"You'll both have to sit in the car the rest of the afternoon while we fish," she said.

Nate watched Fitz climb into the back seat and leave the door open.

"Go on up to the car and wait for Grandpa. Go on now."

In a short time, Grandpa came down the path with two good-sized smallmouth on his stringer. He passed Nate standing at the back of the car and Fitz sitting in the back seat with one leg outside.

"Grandma, I got something for the skillet," he said. He walked sideways down the bank, holding the stringer with the smallmouth bass away from him as he went. When he got to the lake, he put his stringer into the water.

A minute later he came back up to the car. "Why were you screaming bloody murder, Nate?" he asked.

"We were just fooling around."

"What did Fitz do to you?"

"Nothing. We were just wrestling."

"Boys, you can't be horsing around out here. It's dangerous. The only way to make sure you don't kill yourselves is to lock you up in the car. You want that, Fitz?"

"No, sir."

"You want that, Nate?"

"No, sir."

"I can't keep an eye on you two the whole time. Hell, I came out here to fish."

Grandma came up the hill, pushing off her knees with each step.

"Grandpa, you take Fitz around with you and Nate can stay here with me."

"I don't know. Sounds like we're letting them off."

"They'll tear up your back seat if you leave them in the car."

"Hmmm," he said. "Well, let's have some lunch first."

The rest of the afternoon was devoted entirely to catching a good mess of fish. When they got home, the boys watched Grandpa fillet the mess of bluegill first, then the bass and lastly the catfish he had caught. He asked if Fitz wanted to fillet one and Fitz declined. Nate tried, and after that Fitz wanted to try. They were both too timid with the knife to be effective.

Grandma dipped the fillets into cornmeal batter and fried them up with diced potatoes, onions and applesauce for supper. After all the dishes were washed, dried and put away, everyone was too pooped for anything else but sleep.

The next morning, Fitz woke up and shook Nate awake.

"What?" Nate kept his eyes closed.

"Let's go swimming."

"I'm sleeping."

"Come on. We'll get Grandma to take us to Big Rock."

"You think she will?" Nate's eyes were still closed.

"Sure she will. Let's get up and ask."

They got up and went into the kitchen. They could see that Grandma and Grandpa had already had their breakfast. Grandpa had gone into town. Grandma came into the kitchen from the back room and asked the boys what they wanted for breakfast. They both wanted cereal and bacon. Grandma sat at the table with them, watching them chomp the cereal and slurp the milk.

"Well, have you all decided –" she started to say. "Nate, don't slurp your milk, honey. You don't want people to hear you eat. And close your mouth when you chew. That's bad manners. Mercy, you boys."

"Listen to this, Grandma," Fitz said. He took in a big spoonful of cereal and closed his mouth, making no sound except for muffled crunching. He ate very slowly and had to concentrate on keeping his mouth closed the whole time. Nate watched him and decided that if he chewed each bite that slowly he would finish his cereal at about suppertime.

"That's right, Fitz," Grandma said. "Well, boys, have you decided what you want to do today? I thought maybe I'd walk you down to the schoolyard and you two could play ball."

"Can we go swimming after that?" Fitz asked.

"Well, I guess so. Did you-all remember to bring your bathing suits?"

"Yes, ma'am," Fitz said.

"Would you like to go to Cherokee Park?"

"No, Big Rock," Fitz said.

"I'm not taking you to Big Rock. It's too deep out there, and you know I can't swim. You let your dad take you there sometime. He's a good swimmer. Cherokee Park has a nice pool."

"All right," Fitz said. "Big Rock's more fun, though."

"Oh, Cherokee's fun," Grandma said. "Water's water, ain't it? How about it, Nate?"

"I like Cherokee Park," Nate said.

"Ah, you'd be happy in a toilet," Fitz said.

"Hush, Fitz. You're so mean to your little brother," Grandma said. She smacked his hand lightly.

After breakfast, Grandma walked the boys down the alley and across the street to the schoolyard. The boys took turns pitching a tennis ball to each other and belting the ball against the side of the six-story school building. Fitz struck out Nate repeatedly until Grandma made him lob it in so Nate could hit it.

"Your dad used to hit the balls onto the roof," Grandma said. "I bet there are a thousand balls up there."

Fitz hit one just below the top and slung the bat down in anger. Grandma couldn't understand Fitz's reaction.

"Your game would be over if you hit it onto the roof," she said. "I've only got the one ball."

"No, we'd climb up the downspout and get it," Fitz said.

"I'm not letting you climb up there. Your dad would kill me."

At noon, Grandpa returned from downtown, and after lunch he drove Grandma and the boys to Cherokee Park. The pool was crowded, and more than half the kids in the water were black. Fitz and Nate had never been to a pool with black kids before.

The two boys started at the shallow end. The water was too cold at first. They walked to the fountain in the middle and sat down, watching the other kids running and splashing in the shallow end. They went to the five-foot end, where they had to stand on their tippy toes. The water felt good and refreshing.

Once they had dunked their heads under, there was nothing left to be timid about. They sank to the bottom together and then floated to the top. Fitz splashed Nate and laughed. Nate splashed back and Fitz laughed again. He seemed very happy to get shot back.

A black boy dog-paddled over to them. "Hey, do you-all live nearby?" he asked.

"No," Fitz said. "We're up visiting our Grandma and Grandpa. We're from Nicholasville."

"Oh," he said. "Can you stay under water long?"

"Yeah, I guess," Fitz said.

"Bet I can stay under longer than both of you," he said, looking over at Nate.

"OK," Fitz said. "Let's see."

The black boy swam over to the railing and wiped the water from his face. Fitz and Nate followed. They hung on to the rail.

"OK," the boy said. "When I count to three we'll drop to the bottom and see who can stay down the longest. Ready? One. Two. Three."

They all took a deep breath and lifted up from the rail, then dropped down and squatted on the bottom with one hand pressed to the wall and the other flailing in an upward motion to keep them down.

They all had their eyes open and looked at each other. Fitz showed Nate his middle finger. Nate showed Fitz his middle finger. It wasn't long after that that the black boy pinched his nose and started to shake. He pushed off the bottom and went up for air. Nate closed his eyes and concentrated hard to avoid looking at Fitz. Fitz watched the plunge of arms and legs as a swimmer approached and passed. He could see the black boy's feet kicking to the side of him.

Fitz's head tightened and bubbles blew out his nose. He looked at Nate to see if he was straining. Nate's head was bowed as if he were praying. Fitz couldn't hold it any longer. He shoved off the bottom and blew out at the same time. As soon as he breathed in air, Nate came up.

"I win! I win!" Nate screamed.

Fitz caught his breath and then elbowed the black boy, "Come on, let's get him."

Nate shoved off the wall and swam as hard as he could. The black boy grabbed Nate's left ankle, Fitz grabbed his right and they towed him back to the five-foot end.

"Stop it! Let go!" Nate shouted.

Fitz grabbed him by the neck and shoved him under, holding him at the shoulders. He let Nate surface for a second, then shoved him under again. Fitz let him up for a breath of air, then threw him over to the black boy, who dunked him. The black boy let him up and then let go of him. Nate swam to the rail, coughing.

"Don't let him go!" Fitz said to the black boy.

"He slipped out of my hands."

They swam over to Nate and pried his fingers from the rail.

"Don't, Fitz! I can't catch my breath. I'm serious. I can't breathe!"

"Oh, shut up. You can hold your breath better than both of us," Fitz said. He pushed Nate into the arms of the black boy, who dunked him under the water.

"Hold his neck," Fitz said. "He can't squirm that way."

Nate was losing strength fast. The black boy had a good, firm grip on his neck. A black woman in a long cover-up ran along the side of the pool, screaming, "Lamont! Lamont!"

Fitz saw that Nate wasn't squirming any more and laughed. "That's it. That's it."

The kids at the shallow end of the pool stopped playing and watched the black woman running toward the deep end, crying, "Lamont! Lamont!"

Fitz turned around and saw that everyone in the pool was looking at him and that the place had grown quiet. He saw the black woman scampering beside the pool with tears streaming down her cheeks. "Lamont! Lamont!"

Still holding Nate under the water, the black boy turned around and saw his mother at the edge of the pool.

"Let go of that boy!" she screamed.

He let go and Nate sprang up and jumped for the rail. He hung onto the rail and coughed and cried. Everyone in the pool watched in silence. The only sounds were the fountain splashing and Nate coughing and crying.

"Lamont, get your ass out of the pool right now," the woman said, wiping her cheeks.

Lamont swam over to her, lifted himself onto the rail and climbed out.

The kids at the shallow end began moving around and talking again, and everyone went back to playing. Fitz swam over to Nate on the rail and patted him on the back.

"Come on, let's get out for a minute," Fitz said.

Nate moved down the rail away from him and coughed. Nate lifted himself out and walked over to Grandma, who was sitting far away from the pool under a shade tree, reading a book. She heard Nate coughing and looked up at his red face.

"Oh, honey, what's wrong?" she asked. "Did you swallow water?"

Nate coughed and nodded his head. Grandma put a towel around him.

Fitz came running up.

"What happened to Nate, Fitz?"

"Oh, he got into a fight with a black boy," Fitz said.

"I heard a woman screaming after her son. Is that who he was fighting with?"

"Yes," Fitz said.

"Well, Fitz, why didn't you take up for your little brother?"

"I thought they were playing."

Nate cut off his cough and said, "They tried to drown me, Grandma."

"Who did?"

"Oh, he's being silly," Fitz said.

"They did," Nate said. "Fitz and that black boy took turns holding me under water."

"Well, Fitz!"

"We were playing. He knows that."

"You're a fart-face!" Nate shouted.

"Nate! Don't talk like that. My goodness, you boys are more than I can take. I can't believe the two of you are brothers acting the way you do. Grandpa and I are too old to referee you boys. Can't you be civil while you're up here with us?"

Fitz put a towel over his head and sat down with his back to Grandma and Nate.

"Come on, let's walk to the entrance and wait for Grandpa," she said.

They took the narrow path through the park. The path was shaded and cool. Fitz had the towel around his neck and walked a couple steps ahead of the other two. Grandma had her arm around Nate. She wiped his wet hair out of his eyes.

Grandpa pulled up, and after they got in, Fitz and Nate waited for Grandma to tell what had happened at the pool, but she never did. They figured he would hear about it later.

Everyone went through the motions as they ate their dinner. Not much was said. Grandma didn't tell Grandpa what had happened at the pool as far as the boys knew, but Grandpa could sense by the way the boys were ignoring each other at the table that something had probably happened that afternoon.

That night in bed, Nate lay on his back, thinking. He couldn't sleep right away. Fitz was lying on his side with his back to him, breathing heavily through his nose. Nate wanted to tell him he was sorry for making Grandma mad at them, but that he had been truly scared in the pool. He hadn't known what else to do but rat on him.

He wanted Fitz to know that he had been really scared that he was going to drown because he had used up all of his energy in the contest and in fighting them off. When they had held him under he had tried to stay calm so he could stay under longer, but he had panicked and got really scared, and he had been afraid that Fitz and the black boy hadn't realized how serious the situation had become.

He knew they were only playing and meant no harm, but if they had known how scared he was, they would have let him up and given him time to calm down. All he had needed was time to catch his breath.

"Fitz," Nate whispered.

There was no answer.

"Fitz."

No answer.

Nate turned over and closed his eyes, but sleep wouldn't come. *I guess me and Fitz aren't meant to be friends*, he thought. *We just can't seem to get along. It's like he's trying to get rid of me. He's tried to kill me twice. Why would he want to kill his own brother?*

"Fitz, are you trying to kill me?"

"Shut up, butthole."

"Well, are you?"

"Shut up. I'm sleeping."

The next morning was Friday, their last full day in Louisville. Nothing was said about the swimming pool over breakfast, but the boys could tell by Grandpa's silence that he had found out what had happened.

Grandpa moved his gaze from the newspaper to his plate. He usually watched the boys eat and made little cutting remarks or jokes, but this morning there was nothing. He gathered his and Grandma's dirty dishes and washed them. When he turned around to get the boys' dishes and saw they were still eating, he said, "You two can do your own dishes." He dried his hands with the dish towel and walked into the back room.

After breakfast, they drove to a nearby farm to pick blackberries. There wasn't any conversation on the way to the farm, and Nate noticed that Fitz wouldn't even look at him. When they got back home, Grandma walked them to the schoolyard to play ball, but there was no enthusiasm in it. Fitz lobbed the tennis ball repeatedly so Nate could hit it. Nate lobbed the ball back for Fitz, and then they went home.

Nothing much was said on the walk back. Fitz answered all of Grandma's inquiries with a single word, and there was no expression in his voice. After supper, Fitz and Nate sat on the front porch while Grandma and Grandpa cleaned up. No one was on the sidewalk, in the street or outside their house. They heard the screen door click and swing open. Grandma sat next to Nate on the wooden glider. Grandpa sat in the chair next to Fitz.

"Well, boys, I guess tomorrow morning we'll be taking you back home," Grandpa said. "Looking forward to going home, Fitz?"

"No."

"Ah, why not?"

"Got school on Monday."

"Ha, ha," Grandpa laughed. "You're like me. I never cared for school neither. What about you, Nate?"

"I hate it."

"School's good for you boys."

Nothing was said for a while.

"I guess you're looking forward to seeing your ma and pa, eh?" Grandpa said.

"Yeah, I guess," Fitz said.

"Well, we sure enjoy having you boys come up and stay with us. Don't we, Grandma?"

"Yes, we sure do," she drew Nate near and hugged him.

"We hate to have to take you back, but your ma and pa sure would be upset if we kept you too long," Grandpa said.

Grandpa couldn't get Fitz or Nate to talk about anything, and Grandma made matters worse for him by keeping silent along with them.

"Hey, boys," Grandpa said. "The Reds come on in a half-hour. You want to watch them?"

"Sure," Fitz said.

Everyone went inside. Grandma measured out a small amount of soda for the boys and let them take it into the living room.

The Reds were trailing the Giants 7-0 in the fourth inning when Fitz and Nate went off to bed. Grandma came into the room after they were tucked in and kissed them goodnight. She clicked the light off and pulled the door to, so that it was pitch black in the room. They lay on their backs, and neither one moved or stirred for about an hour. Finally, Nate turned so he had his back to Fitz and tried to sleep.

Fitz lay on his back with his eyes open. He wasn't sleepy. "Nate," he said.

"Yeah."

"I had a dream about us."

"Already?" Nate turned over.

"No, knothead. Last night."

Nate was happy Fitz was talking to him again. He could call him knothead, butthole, dickface, anything so long as he was talking to him.

"What was it about?"

"You remember when we rode our bikes up Beacon Hill and we reached the top and then coasted down the hill and we started racing and we were going too fast?"

"Yeah."

"Well, last night in my dream it was just like that. It was so real, too. We were going up the hill and I said to you, 'This is impossible. We're in Louisville right now.' And you said, 'Let's try and make it home and see if Mom and Dad are surprised to see us.'

"We reached the top of the hill and started coasting down, picking up speed. Then you started pedaling and pulled out in front and I beat my pedals and caught up to you. We were going way too fast. I was really worried but you kept on pedaling and got out ahead of me again. I yelled at you to slow down, but you wouldn't.

"I caught up to you and kicked your back tire and we both lost balance. You crashed and rolled under a parked car, and I veered off into Jarrett's front yard and crashed in the grass. My knee hurt real bad. I looked across the street and saw your bike underneath the front of a car. I limped over to the car and looked under it, but only your bike was there.

"I said, 'Nate! Nate!' and you said, 'Hey, Fitz, I'm up here.' I turned around, but I still couldn't see you. You said, 'Look up.' I looked up and you were kind of floating in the air above the car. You were like a ghost 'cause I could see through your skin. I said, 'Nate, what are you doing up there?' And you said, 'I've got to go that way,' and you pointed to the sky. 'No,' I said. 'I don't want you to go.' 'It's OK, Fitz,' you said. 'I'm all right.'"

Fitz stopped at that point in the story.

"Then what?" Nate asked. "What else happened?"

Fitz didn't answer. He swallowed and then turned over.

Nate lay on his back to think. There was no way he could sleep now. He wished there was a way he could get into that dream and come back down to the ground and show Fitz he was all right.

So Fitz doesn't want to kill me after all, he thought. *To have a dream like that and get upset retelling it means he must really care about me. Even if we can't get along, I guess we can still care about each other.*

If you want to get an automatic email when Jonathan's next book is released, sign up here (bit.ly/1BYvXx5).

You will only be contacted when a new book is released, your address will never be shared, and you can unsubscribe at any time.

Please consider leaving a review of On Your Own at Amazon. Even if it's only a sentence or two, your comment would be very helpful.

Amazon US: (http://www.amazon.com/dp/B00W1UUDNG/)

Amazon UK: (http://www.amazon.co.uk/dp/B00W1UUDNG/)

Made in the USA
Middletown, DE
23 June 2015